Bound

This book is a work of fiction. Names, characters, places, and incidents are the product of the author's imagination or are used fictitiously. Any resemblance to actual events, locales, or persons, living or dead, is coincidental.

Cover Design: C. Wehmhoefer
Interior Illustrations: C. Wehmhoefer
Editing: Enchanted Ink Publishing
Book Design and Typesetting: Enchanted Ink Publishing

The text type was set in EB Garamond

ISBN: 979-8-9914418-8-9 (E-book)
ISBN: 979-8-218-48451-4 (Paperback)
ISBN: 979-8-9914418-9-6 (Hardcover)
ISBN: 979-8-991-4418-7-2 (Audiobook)

Thank you for your support of the author's rights.

WWW.CWEHMHOEFER.COM

DISCLAIMER

This novel contains descriptions of intense forms of delusion and psychotic behavior. This novel also includes stalking and obsession, which could be upsetting and disturbing to some readers. Read with caution.

This novel does not condone stalking; stalking is against the law.

If you are being threatened, intimidated, or stalked, please contact your local authorities or reach out to the resources below.

Victim Connect:
1-855-4VICTIM(1-855-484-2846)

National Domestic Violence Hotline:
1-800-799-7233 or TTY 1-800-787-3224 en Español

National Sexual Assault Hotline:
1-800-656-HOPE (4673)

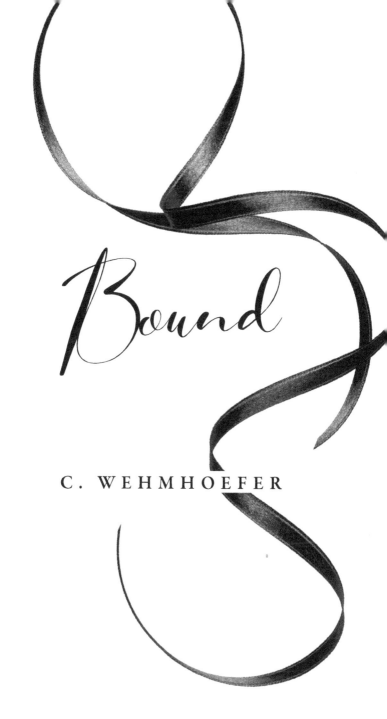

Bound

C. WEHMHOEFER

Prologue

HER HEART THUNDERED IN HER CHEST AS HER feet pounded against the wet ground. The mud sucked at her heels, trying to trap her. Adrenaline rushed through her veins like an electric current prickling her skin. A crippling fear gripped her; she couldn't see merely a few feet in front of her. The cold night grasped at her, holding on to her with its cold pale fingers.

She had to think of her escape, to keep her mind on the present moment. She needed to gain ground faster; her life depended on it. The cold air stung her lungs as she panted her way through the thick brush of the midnight forest.

She didn't know how long she'd been gone or how long she'd been knocked out; all she knew was that she had escaped. Hopefully she could get a head start away from her captor.

There was no time to remove or even loosen the rope rubbing her wrists raw. Even now, the rough material licked at her skin, burning it with a heat she hadn't felt before. Her plan was to remove the rope as soon as she knew she was far enough away or had the chance to stop.

Her mind raced. She didn't know where she was or who had brought her here. She'd awoken in the darkness with her hands tethered together in front of her, the smell of dank earth in the air.

As she ran, her lungs burned. She'd been running in the dark woods for what felt like hours. The branches ripping past her clawed into her skin. Trees scratched her, and warm blood dripped down her arms and face. The salt of her sweat stung the tiny abrasions, but she couldn't stop; she had to keep going.

She was frantic with thoughts of how she was going to survive the night, assuming she didn't get caught or, even worse, killed by her captor.

In a flash, she tripped on an overgrown root jutting out from the damp earth. Falling to her knees, she barely caught herself with her constrained hands. She yelped at the sharp pain in her ankle and knew she had sprained or broken it. As she reached for her ankle, she noticed a flickering light, a flashlight running in her direction.

Her worst fear was realized: her captor was chasing her. Hopelessness and pure intoxicating fear gripped her heart.

She had two options: keep running on her injured leg or hide as best she could in the cold dark forest. She reached down to her ankle. When she tried to move it, burning pain flooded her once more. Tears started to streak down her face, and she held back a scream. There was no choice but to hide.

Clawing her fingers into the soft earth, she dragged herself to a large tree, biting the insides of her cheeks to prevent herself from screaming out in pain. The tree she reached had a large overgrown root that was just big enough for her to hide under. She curled herself into the mangled root. Lying still for a brief moment, she leaned against her only protection, Mother Nature. She then began pulling fallen leaves and sticks around her legs, trying to conceal herself as best she could. The cold earth clumped under her nails; the ground felt like heavy clay sticking to everything.

She looked up for a moment. The light was coming closer.

With the stillness of the night surrounding her, she listened for footsteps closing in. She breathed slowly, letting the cold air wash over her. The flashlight shined in the distance, illuminating the leaves on the blackened trees. The light was slowly getting brighter and brighter; her captor was coming closer with every moment.

Fear burned her lungs. She was paralyzed, unable to move. It felt as if her soul were trying to tear itself free, itching and clawing at her skin in an attempt to leave her tattered body behind. She tried to calm herself, taking shallow silent breaths, being sure not to move a muscle.

As she lay in the darkness, watching the swaying flashlight flicker on the trees, approaching steps crunched the broken branches lying dormant on the forest floor. Her captor was getting close. Her heart pounded harder in her chest, moving upward to her throat, nearly choking her. She held back her fear as tears streamed down her face like a raging river.

She wasn't sure if she was going to make it through the night. The thought of her life ending was crippling to her. She had so much to live for: her son, her family, her career.

Her nose started to run, but she resisted the urge to sniffle. Holding herself closer to the tree, she pushed her bound hands practically inside her stomach.

The footsteps came closer and closer. They couldn't be more than ten feet away. She held her breath. Her eyes followed the path of the flashlight, which seemed to be scouting the entire forest for her. The footsteps moved closer, and she could hear the pure weight of the person stepping toward her. They were so close. The light from the flashlight suddenly seemed so bright. They were standing directly behind her. Her heartbeat seemed to freeze, muting itself in her chest; she didn't dare breathe.

The large root she was hiding under shifted. The person was standing directly on top of her. Then something snapped a branch in the distance. The root shifted again as her pursuer stepped backward, chasing the same noise she'd heard. Their footsteps pattered off into the distance.

She waited before she let out her breath. They were gone. She tilted her head to look for the light from the flashlight, but all she saw was the still, dark forest. A wave of appreciation washed over her; maybe she would live through this.

She decided to finally remove the rope from around her wrists. Repositioning her weight to move her hands to her mouth, she bit into the coarse material, trying to free herself.

Without warning, a thud shook the ground. Someone had jumped over the root and landed in front of her. Lying before them, she looked up to find their dark eyes staring straight into her.

She let out an earth-shattering scream. As she screamed, their large hands wrapped around her neck, smothering her voice in the dark night. She pulled and scratched at the thick long sleeves that covered their forearms. She desperately clawed as their heavy weight pushed her into the damp earth. She looked at the person smothering her airway, but she couldn't see their face in the darkness.

Anger was evident in the force they exerted onto her neck and the throaty growls coming from their struggle with her. Her lungs burned for air. She gasped, kicking and writhing on the wet forest floor. The last bit of life in her fluttered like a butterfly lost in the wind. She kicked as much as she could, but her legs became weak, and her arms went limp. Her eyes closed, and there was only darkness.

One

REESE HAD KNOWN ABOUT BLUE SKY, COLORADO, for as long as she could remember. Her father had loved taking drives along the winding mountain roads. Although the torture of looking off the side of the cliffs in a fast-moving station wagon had always made Reese shiver in fear, her father had loved taking the corners close and fast.

Reese remembered the first time she'd driven into Blue Sky; the name of the town did it justice in most cases. The sky here was the deepest blue, with large billowing white clouds that always seemed to hug the steep cliffs of the surrounding mountaintops. The town of Blue Sky was nestled into a rolling mountainside. It almost seemed to be sandwiched between two giants.

Reese drove past the welcome sign to Blue Sky, which boasted a population of just under six thousand. She'd always questioned why people moved to this small, almost desolate town.

She reminisced about her memory of Blue Sky and meeting her childhood friend, Gina.

Reese had done some major convincing to get her father and mother to stop at the town's soda shop. Looking back, the reason they'd stopped was probably to halt her whining in the back seat. She remembered walking into the shop, the old Western swinging doors roaring with a familiar creaking noise as she pushed past them. Reese had pinpointed the smell of sugar rushing through the shop. Her young eyes had widened at all the sugary possibilities, taking in every sweet treat that adorned the walls. The look on her face must have made it apparent that she was lost in a sugary heaven.

The old clerk behind the counter watched with an old cracked smile as Reese froze in place, taking everything in. The clerk was helping a girl sitting at the aged bar top. The girl asked the clerk to create a strange dessert float that consisted of sarsaparilla, vanilla, and blackberry. Reese shyly walked up to the counter, her eyes wide as she looked at all the flavors so nicely placed on the large shelves behind the bar top. Overwhelmed and simply in awe, Reese just stood there in silence. Meanwhile, the clerk had been asking Reese what she wanted for a few moments.

Gina, the young blond girl sitting at the counter, being the master of the situation like she always was, stated, "She'll have one of these," motioning to the drink in front of her.

Reese had turned blankly to Gina, who sat sipping the float the man had made for her. Gina had motioned for Reese to sit on the chair next to her, and Reese had warily obliged.

From that time on, Reese and Gina made it a point to always see each other when Reese and her family passed through town. Gina and Reese's friendship was what had convinced Reese to move to Blue Sky.

Having been a city dweller for the last twenty-five years, Reese had a few nervous butterflies in her stomach. She hoped she'd be able to fit in with the rural crowd. Blue Sky wasn't for those who didn't know how to ride a horse or fix a tractor.

As thoughts rolled over in her head, she looked back to the midnight-black 1968 Barracuda she was towing behind her moving truck. Reese knew that if she didn't fit in with her gallery, her classic car, which she and her father had painstakingly built, would surely make it easier to be seen as a local—at least, she hoped so.

When it came down to it, Reese was moving to Blue Sky for a new start. She had been lucky enough to be able to afford moving out of Denver due to her art sales.

Reese had safeguarded her paintings for years before entering an art show in Denver. Like most things in life, Reese had thought her first art show was going to be a flop. One painting of an abstract oil spill over a woman had caught the attention of several notable art buyers who'd been browsing the show. Reese had received a call from a buyer who wanted to commission an entire line of her work for a hefty million dollars in profit. Even now, Reese was blown away that she was lucky enough to have been noticed. Things like this didn't just happen. It was this whirlwind of fate that had brought her here to chase her dreams of buying the soda shop she'd grown up loving and revamping it into a morning tea joint with hopes of selling and showing her art on the side.

Reese had been in contact with a local real estate agent, Michael Gavinthal, and he'd facilitated the purchase. Michael had been skeptical that a Denverite would want an old shop on the main street of a small town, but Reese's cash offer had prompted him to take her seriously.

Reese rolled down the main street with her moving truck and Barracuda in tow. She spotted the old Soda Fountain building, with its bright blue paint peeling under the mountain sun. Reese slowly pulled up in front of the building, and as she did, she noticed a flash of white and felt the wind rip through the tiny crack in the window. Reese jumped as a paper hit the windshield.

The paper read "Missing" in bold red letters and had a picture of a gorgeous young blond woman with pale pink lips and sun-kissed skin. Reese's heart sank.

That poor woman, she thought.

She read the flyer from the inside of her car.

Hannah Franklin, a longtime resident of Blue Sky, had gone missing a little over a month ago. No one had seen her since. She'd last been seen working her shift at her hardware shop.

Reese hoped Hannah had wandered away from Blue Sky to see what else the world could offer. A town like this didn't seem like it could handle a beautiful woman like Hannah.

Reese shook herself out of her whirlwind of thoughts about the missing woman. She reached for the door handle and hopped out of the moving truck before grabbing the flyer from her windshield. It felt like it would be an act of sacrilege to throw the flyer into the trash, so Reese held on to it as she walked up to the Soda Fountain.

The old saloon doors were still intact, but now they were pinned to the side of the doorway, a memory of the past just brushed to the side. Reese pushed open the shop doors that were in place of the saloon doors and noted the new ones still had the old wooden squeak, oh so similar to the squeak of the saloon doors she'd pushed open the day she met Gina.

Inside, there was the lingering smell of dust and slight decay—not of organic matter, but of the building. It had a distinct musky scent. Her gaze landed on a man in a long-sleeve button-down shirt and jeans. He was on his cell phone with his back turned to Reese.

He must be Michael, she thought. His hair was dark and cleanly cut around his neck. As Michael turned, she noticed that his eyes were a hazel green with honey-colored specks showing through. His jawline was sharp, and he had small dimples in each cheek.

Michael saw Reese standing at the entrance and quickly concluded his call. His dress shoes echoed as he crossed the wooden floor.

"You must be Reese. It's so nice to finally meet you." Michael held his toned arm out, and when Reese shook his hand, she noticed his skin was cold to the touch.

"Nice to meet you, Michael. Thank you so much for being so understanding about this buy," Reese stated as she slid her hand out of his.

"Oh, of course. I have to say, it's very rare that we get full cash offers 'round here." His voice was tinged with a slight drawl.

Reese chuckled softly. "I guess I'm just a bit old-fashioned that way. I like to keep things simple."

Michael raised an eyebrow, clearly intrigued. "Well, that's refreshing. It definitely makes the process smoother. Have you been looking for a place for a while?"

Reese shook her head. "Not too long. I knew of this old place from a distant childhood memory. When I saw it was on the market, it just felt right. Sometimes life brings you to the right place at the right time, you know?"

"Absolutely," Michael agreed, nodding. "Finding the perfect fit can be a bit like finding a needle in a haystack. But when it clicks, it clicks."

After they worked out the final details of her recent buy, Reese signed the last of the seemingly never-ending stack of paperwork. "I appreciate you making this so straightforward, Michael. It's been a pleasure working with you."

"Likewise, Reese. If you ever need anything or have any questions down the line, don't hesitate to reach out," Michael said, handing her a business card with a smile.

Reese took the card, her expression warm. "Will do. Thanks again for everything."

Michael thumbed through the stack of paperwork that had sat so dignified on the old bar top. He warmly congratulated her, "Good luck with the new place! I hope it brings you all the happiness you're looking for."

Reese flashed Michael a genuine smile. "Thanks, Michael. I'm sure it will." Reese began to inspect the shop; her eyes immediately settled on the tall bar top covered in a thin layer of dust. The same bar top Reese had once sat at as a child, adoring the colorful flavor additives and strange creations Gina had insisted the worker make for her.

As Reese reminisced about how the shop had looked in her past, she let her eyes wander around the room. The dark-wood shelves and old curved 1800s bar top looked exactly the same as when she was a kid, just a little more ragged. The edges of the bar top were worn, and the wood had faded to nearly gray. The space seemed empty without the small tables that had been there last time she was there. Reese planned to bring in old crushed-velvet couches and armchairs, as well as bistro-style tables and chairs.

Reese looked at the blank white walls in the back. That space must have been an old stockroom. Now it was going to be the home of the gallery she was planning on opening. Reese had a tinge of doubt regarding whether the people of Blue Sky would accept her art or if they would judge her for its raw nature. Although she knew art at its core was meant to be judged, she didn't want that judgment to follow her as a person, especially in such a small town.

Michael had finished up with the final details of the purchase and handed Reese the key to the shop. Reese's hand drooped as the full weight of the skeleton key hit her palm. It was the original key for the 1800s building. She started imagining her new shop in its full glory, but before she could sink deeper into her fantasy, Michael's voice brought her back to the present.

"You know, there's no better way to get to know the town you just moved to than by checking out the local bar." He swallowed. "I wouldn't mind buying you a drink to celebrate."

Reese smiled warmly at him. "I might have to take you up on the offer. But I should get a few things moved in;

that way I can feel like I have something real to celebrate. It still doesn't seem real."

"If you'd like some help, let me know. I am more than willing to lend a helping hand 'round here," Michael offered.

"Oh, I am sure I can manage, but thank you. I might swing by that bar though," Reese stated, bringing the conversation back to the bar. Secretly, she didn't want his help moving her things in; she had her boundaries. After all, she also had just met the man.

"Correction, the *only* bar in this small town," Michael retorted. "What time can I expect you?"

"I am not really sure." Reese was starting to pick up on his stubbornness. She could see why he was the only real estate agent in town; he was very pushy. She smiled at Michael awkwardly.

"Well, you know I'll be watching for you. I hope you can make it." Just like that, Michael gathered the stack of papers and turned toward the door. Relief washed over Reese as Michael congratulated her again and stepped out of the shop. Michael was one she would have to watch out for; he seemed like he had gotten his sales and his social tactics from a used-car lot. He was determined.

Two

REESE SPENT THE NEXT FEW HOURS MOVING MOST of the necessities into the Soda Fountain. She had also taken care of the essentials of the building—and she managed to turn the water and gas back on, something she hadn't even thought about. She'd even had to look up a manual on how to light the pilot light. The thought of doing all the basic upkeep of the building alone made her proud to say this was her building and new home now.

The entrance was littered with boxes of her personal items as well as shop items, like her loose-leaf teas, some of her homegrown herbs and spices, and other curiosities for her new business. Reese was still playing with the idea of having an art gallery near the rear of the store, where she would feature her art in a clean, tasteful display. She'd brought many of her art pieces with her, and she still had even more items to unload.

Reese left her moving truck parked in front of the shop while she unhitched her 'Cuda and parked it in the rear of the building, where she could see it from her upstairs apartment. The upstairs apartment was complete with an old woodburning stove and a giant stained glass window that made the room light up with brilliant colors throughout the day.

Feeling overwhelmed by the mess of the place, she thought of going to the bar—the *only* bar. *I could use a drink*, she thought. The strange notion of seeing Michael there crossed her mind. There was something about Michael that she couldn't put her finger on. Had Michael been flirting, or attempting to flirt with Reese before? Well, at least he'd waited until she had finished signing the deed. Yes, Reese was going to the bar. She needed a reward for following her path.

Just as Reese was making her way back inside her shop, a familiar face slid in front of her.

"Gina!" Reese said excitedly. Reese and Gina hugged for a moment before Reese invited Gina inside the shop.

"Wow, it looks exactly the same as when we were kids," Gina said as she looked around, taking in the nostalgia with Reese. "The only thing this place is missing is the old man we nearly tortured making the odd drinks." Gina let out a quiet chuckle.

Gina had grown so much within the last few years. Although her hair had once been a bright blond, it had darkened to an ash blond that now shaped the side of her face in a tight bob. One thing that hadn't changed was Gina's dark hazel eyes, which made even her ash-toned hair seem brighter than it truly was.

Just having Gina around seemed to make the shop come to life. That was the effect Gina had on everyone and everything around her—she was the life of the party. Gina was experienced at getting the party to follow her everywhere she went and was what most would call a functioning alcoholic, but in these small towns, it seemed to be the norm to drink before eleven in the morning.

"I can't wait to turn this town upside down with you." Gina threw a bright smile at Reese.

Reese recalled the last time she had seen Gina. Gina had visited her in Denver, where for four nights Gina had convinced Reese that debauchery was life. Although Reese felt a forever connection to Gina, she knew her friend was only good in small doses.

"Let's go grab a drink," Gina suggested.

"Funny you should suggest that—is this bar the only form of entertainment around here?" Reese already knew the answer.

"You know, there aren't a lot of things to do in this town, so most of us wash our boredom down with our friends Jack, Jim, or even Jameson," Gina retorted.

The light push from Gina had fully convinced her to go to the bar, which only the locals knew of and frequented.

Reese's nerves were on edge. She was going out for the first time in a very long time.

Well, what the hell. What could happen besides some stumbling rednecks and unsavory country mountain folk? she thought.

With one push of the heavy door, she knew she was in for a night of fun. The smell of the bar was heavy, like musky moist cabin logs. A humid fire was roaring in the background, and on top of the smoke was the smell of stale beer. The walls were wood paneled, the same paneling you'd find in an outdated home from the seventies when shag carpet was all the rage.

Reese moved forward to the bar top, which was well taken care of, the wood shiny and smooth to the touch. The backdrop of the bar was old-timey Western, with a mirror speckled black along the edges.

Reese slid onto a padded barstool with Gina standing beside her. But when Gina spotted a few regulars, she moved away from Reese and into the crowd of the bar. The crowded bar was full of white hair and long beards, with a few younger patrons sprinkled in for good measure. She'd expected a younger crowd; it was a bar, after all. But as the thought dawned on her, she realized this was likely the only form of entertainment in this dying mining town.

The bartender, who was leaning against the bar, turned his head, his long sandy-blond hair pulled to the base of his neck, and scowled at Reese. Then he turned back to his buddy, who was howling with laughter among some older men in the corner.

Yup, small town all right. Well, Reese knew exactly what to do: pull a page out of Gina's book.

She moved from her barstool and walked behind the bar. Stares burned into her skin. She turned, found the shot glasses, grabbed the tequila from the bar, and poured herself a shot. Then Reese placed the bottle on the bar top, walked to the other side of the counter, and sat.

The bartender glared in her direction. Reese knew this could go two ways: either cops would be called or these people might laugh. She hoped for the latter. She shot the tequila, and the burn of the alcohol erupted down her throat. She gently placed the shot glass on the bar top. Without losing the attention of the men in the corner, Reese put a twenty-dollar bill down. She looked to the bartender, who had now metaphorically dropped his jaw on the ground. He looked at this bold woman. The bartender shifted his weight and moved slowly in her direction, his eyes fixated on her. He walked up to her and looked at the twenty-dollar bill.

"Looks like you're already ahead of the game—guess I'll just add it to your tab and my list of 'things I didn't get to do today.'" The bartender's voice crackled over her. The little jab made Reese smile.

"In that case, I'll have another," Reese said, holding his gaze.

Without breaking her stare, the bartender poured her another shot, grabbed a second glass, and poured one for himself.

"You must be Gina's friend," he growled under his breath. Reese wasn't sure if that was meant to be a jab at Gina. He took the other glass and shot the tequila to the back of his throat. "Name's Cody," he croaked in his raspy tequila-burned voice.

Cody was a large man who towered over her and looked like he was built for manual labor or spent seven days a week in the gym. But knowing full well there was no gym in Blue Sky, Reese speculated he was a contractor or miner during the day and a bartender at night.

Cody smirked in Reese's direction before walking back across the bar to his boisterous regulars, who were now staring at Reese.

Reese smiled to herself, then realized the bar had lit up with conversation. It was getting louder, and she let her gaze wander across the patrons. The couple in the corner had no issues with public displays of, well, she wouldn't call it *affection*. Maybe *arousal* was a better word for their ass groping and tangled tongues. With a jolt, Reese noticed it wasn't just any woman—it was Gina. She'd found her plaything for the night.

Good for her, Reese thought as she breathed in the stale air.

One of the gray-bearded men Cody had been chatting with slowly made his way around the room, speaking with each man who came in. He was probably talking about the latest deals on cattle or the best ways to escape the tourists who found themselves in the area.

Reese noticed a burly man nursing a bottle near the deep green pool table. He was wearing the typical flannel shirt you'd see on old Abercrombie ads, the ones that made even the straightest man think of questioning his sexuality, all to get one night with one of the models. He wasn't the model type though; he looked like he'd been working long shifts on an oil rig or something of the sort. He had clean-cut dark hair and light eyes. Reese noted he seemed to be playing pool by himself; he seemed content though. His light eyes peeked up from the pool game for a flash, just long enough for Reese to note he had the lightest blue eyes she had ever seen.

Reese stared at the man, who seemed to be the soft-spoken type. Each time she caught a wisp of his voice in the busy room, she thought it sounded like a warm honey butter washing over the conversations in the now-rowdy bar.

Reese finally had the wherewithal to grab the shot the bartender had poured earlier. She reached for the glass, but Gina, in a staggering blunder, seized the shot from Reese. In one clunky motion, the tequila was down Gina's throat. Gina set the shot glass down and motioned for Cody to pour them another round. This time Cody seemed more perturbed.

Reese gathered he didn't like Gina as he stalked over, poured the shots silently, and walked directly back without making eye contact with Gina. She might have even seen a slight grimace run across Cody's face.

She clinked glasses with Gina and took the shot like a pro. When she put down the glass, she noticed her real estate agent, Michael. He smiled from across the bar and held his glass up to her. Reese did her best to smile back at him, but on the inside, she was dreading talk to Michael again.

Reese continued to watch as the man Gina was with strutted out of the restroom, still zipping up his pants. He walked up behind Gina, grabbed her ass, and went in for a slobbering wet kiss. Gina was shocked at first, but when his mouth met hers, she melted in his arms.

Reese called Cody over, ignoring the awkward situation playing out right beside her.

"You want another?" he said in his rough voice.

Reese wanted to avoid Gina and her plaything making fools of themselves. She needed an excuse to look away from the somewhat-horrific display of affection. Reese carried on with the bartender, asking for the final bill. She was anxious to leave. Bars had never been her scene. She wasn't a partier, and part of her was still reeling from being so bold in front of Cody. At her core, Reese didn't want to put out the image that she was part of this town's delinquent society.

Cody, in his cloudy tone, told Reese the final damage of the night. She thanked him with a nod and a smile, then put some extra cash on the bar to cover the drinks and tip. Reese asked for a glass of water before she intended to leave. As Reese sipped her water, she studied who else was here tonight. The only good thing about going out to the bar was people-watching.

There was a man in the corner, dressed a bit more upscale for this bar, which wasn't saying much. He wore a collared shirt and had his dark hair tied behind his neck. Her gaze must have burned him, because his dark eyes met hers. Electricity hit her arms, a jolt of a strange sensation hit her chest. The man looked away from her and went back to his beer, disinterested in her attention. He stared at the beer on the table as if mesmerized by the bubbles. He looked like the type who wanted to be left alone in his quiet mind.

Reese turned away, grabbing her water, still shaking off the weird feeling that man gave her. She took a sip before her attention fell to Gina, who was stumbling to the restroom. Something about it felt wrong. After looking at the man sitting alone, Reese wasn't sure if he'd made her intuition go into high drive. Trusting her gut, she made her way to the restroom.

When Reese walked inside, her eyes immediately went to the floor inside one of the stalls. Gina's black leather boots were sticking out of the stall, and she was collapsed on the floor.

Three

REESE YANKED THE FLIMSY STALL DOOR OPEN, breaking the lock. She picked up Gina's head, which had been pressed against the cold tile in the restroom. Gina had thrown up on her black leather jacket, and she'd even soiled herself. Reese held Gina's head and tried to get her to come around. Gina's eyes were rolled back into her head, and beads of sweat glistened on her forehead in the fluorescent lights. Just in time, a woman in a green dress opened the restroom door.

"Get Cody!" Reese demanded.

The woman shoved the door back open and ran out, yelling for Cody. Gina started to come through her haze. Her words were slurred, and Reese hushed her and assured her she was okay. She grabbed some toilet paper from the stall, using it to wipe the sweat from Gina's face and the puke from her mouth. Cody rushed in.

"Oh, what the fuck," he growled before running promptly out of the restroom, Reese heard him yelling for a man name "Shance." The panic in Cody's voice lingered in the air; something about Cody being frantic didn't sit well with Reese. Cody didn't seem like the type to let his emotions show.

Reese knew Gina could handle her drinks. It was very unlike her to puke her guts out, let alone to pass out on the bathroom floor. Reese had held Gina's hair back more times than she could count; it was an unspoken bonding moment between girlfriends. But Gina didn't lose her stomach anymore. She was a practiced alcoholic, after all.

"Where am I?" Gina's voice rasped over Reese's ears.

"You're at the bar, I am here, we are getting help," Reese attempted to reassure Gina.

"Who are you?" Gina's voice was muffled in confusion, her eyes glossy, looking strangely toward Reese.

Baffled, Reese stared into Gina's eyes. It's me, Reese. Your friend. Remember the Soda Fountain?"

Just as Gina started to come through, her eyes rolled back. In one motion, Gina's head fell and vomit spilled from her pale lips. Reese suspected mentioning the Soda Fountain sent Gina's gut into a hurling frenzy. Reese moved Gina, angling her toward the toilet, trying to keep her from puking on herself more.

Reese noted Gina's strange delusion that she thought she was somewhere else and didn't recognize Reese. That convinced her that Gina had been drugged.

Before Reese knew it, she was in a restroom filled with four men: Cody, the man in the flannel—who turned out to be wearing a shiny old badge that said "Sheriff" on his hip and a Glock at his lower back—and two volunteer fire-fighters. This town wasn't big enough for an actual fire department, but that meant this community was a tight-knit crowd. Everyone knew everyone's business, so Gina getting drugged would probably play out in the newspaper. Good thing Reese had nothing to hide.

Reese was pushed out of the restroom by the firefighters. She reluctantly left her friend in the tiny bathroom with the four men.

Reese pulled Cody aside. "Does this happen a lot?" she asked. It seemed like a stupid question to ask a bartender, but she didn't know how to react to this situation.

"Hell no, this shit doesn't happen in my bar. And I want to keep it that way," he growled before stalking off in a fuming rage.

He's a real piece of work, Reese thought. But she couldn't blame him; she wouldn't want her bar to have a reputation like that, especially in such a small town.

She watched the restroom eagerly, watching as the sheriff pushed open the door. Reese tried to move her head around the burly sheriff, peeking through the crack of the door to make sure Gina was okay. The sheriff blocked her view as he walked up to Reese.

"Ma'am, I have to ask you some questions," he stated matter-of-factly. He pulled a small notebook from his pocket and thumbed through it.

Reese thought it was strangely odd for an off-duty officer to carry a notebook around. *I guess he wants to always be prepared. Still, very strange.*

"Of course." Reese nodded, and the sheriff directed her outside. When she stepped out of the bar, the chilled mountain air surrounded her.

Reese turned to face the sheriff. He introduced himself as Shance. An odd name for such a burly man. Shance asked basic informational questions before he asked her about Gina and the strange happenings tonight.

"Who was Gina here with?"

Reese didn't know how to answer the question. She did her best to tell the sheriff who Gina was here with, then told him she wouldn't be as much help as some of the regulars could be. The regulars would know Gina's plaything—who, Reese noticed, hadn't been seen in a while—by name. Reese had noticed the regulars weren't too friendly with Shance. After all, he seemed to have been here alone before the drama started. She still hoped they would give him some information. Someone in that bar knew who had drugged Gina. But she speculated locals would want to protect themselves, even if they were breaking the law.

Which could lead a small-town sheriff to suspect the new woman in town had caused the chaos that had just ensued. The very thought sent Reese into a spiral. This wasn't how she wanted to be seen. This wasn't her fault, and she didn't stand for such nefarious acts. Someone in this bar was responsible for drugging her friend, which angered Reese.

The sheriff tilted his head. "Gina was drugged; do you have any idea who could have gotten her drinks?"

Reese shook her head as the cold night air crept up behind her, wrapping her in its cold grip. Reese crossed her arms in an attempt to stay warm. Shance seemed to notice.

"Sorry, Miss Reese. I'll let you go back inside. You look like you're cold." He held the door open for her, and just as she stepped back inside, he handed her his card. "If you think of anything, please give me a call. There have been some concerns about our community's safety in recent days." He was alluding to the missing woman—Reese was sure of it.

Reese took his card in her cold hands; it read "Sheriff S. Brown" in shiny black print.

"Thank you again, Reese." Shance nodded as he stepped back toward the restroom to check on Gina.

Before Reese could put the sheriff's card in her pocket, Cody stepped toward her.

"Well, you just brought the fun tonight, Miss . . . ?"

Who was she kidding the whole town was going to know her sooner or later, right?

"Reese Adler. I own the old Soda Fountain building now," Reese said, once again crossing her arms, feeling a strange wave of uncertainty.

"Oh, shit. Well, I guess a welcome is in order." Cody flashed her a devilish smile that could have melted any other woman's heart.

Reese already knew to steer clear of Cody; he seemed the type to use her for her body for a night and then throw her away with the rest of the trash. Had Gina ever experienced Cody? Most likely.

Reese pushed off the bar and decided to see if the fire-fighters and sheriff would let her check on Gina.

When she entered the restroom, one volunteer fire-fighter was finishing up grabbing vitals, and Gina looked like pure death. Tiny beads of sweat glittered her face; her lips had lost their color. Reese felt her stomach drop, thinking of her friend looking more pale than a translucent ghost. Reese peered into Gina's eyes, the deep red veins surrounding her green hazel irises', the contrast between the colors made her eyes look reptilian. Her eyes were beyond bloodshot; Reese had never seen anything like it.

"Are you going to be okay?" Reese asked.

"Yeah, I'll be fine," Gina rasped.

"Are you sure?" she asked again, but Gina just nodded. "Well, if you need a place to stay tonight, you can crash on my couch."

Gina shook her head. Reese turned for the exit.

"Actually . . ." Gina hung her head in shame. "Can I stay with you until I know that it wasn't my date who drugged me?"

Reese responded with pleasure; after all, Gina was the only family Reese really had in this town. Plus, it would be better for Reese to have someone stay the night with her for the first night.

A few moments later, Gina walked out of the restroom on her own—mostly. The firefighter helped her to the entrance, where Reese was waiting. Gina stumbled, latching on to the doorframe.

"Are you sure you're going to be okay?" Reese asked as she looked at Gina's deathly face. Gina nodded, then pushed past Reese to puke outside.

Reese ran outside to hold Gina's hair away from her face as she continued to puke in the street on her knees.

The sheriff walked outside. "You need some help getting her home?"

Reese nodded. "I don't think she'll make it to my shop in one piece. Thank you."

They helped Gina to her feet and loaded her into the sheriff's truck.

"Well, I guess I have to thank you for taking her in. I'm glad there are some good people out there," the sheriff said. Gina started to fall asleep in the back, which was to be expected, given what the firefighters had said. The firefighters were kind enough to lend a few words of advice to Reese. They asked that she stay hydrated and monitored for the next twenty-four hours, or even upward of the next few days. They instructed Reese to call the police—or in this case, Shance—if Gina appeared to be getting worse. Although the firefighters had urged Gina to go to the hospital, she'd refused.

They pulled up in front of Reese's new shop, and Reese stepped out. The sheriff rushed to the passenger's side, opened Gina's door, and grabbed her, cradling her in his arms. Reese felt a strange bite of jealousy and instantly regretted it. She would want to be in a man's arms like that, just not in this situation.

Reese unlocked the shop door and held it open for the sheriff. He carried Gina to the couch, which Reese had moved in earlier. After shutting the door, she grabbed a few blankets and covered Gina, adding a pillow behind her head.

As Reese tucked Gina into the couch, her eyes drifted to the sheriff, whose gaze was meandering around the shop.

"Thank you again," she said, drawing his attention to her as she stepped behind the curved bar top. Reese followed the sheriff's eyes, which lingered on the flyer of the missing woman that was sitting out on the counter.

"How long has she been missing?" Reese inquired, attempting to make small talk as she watched Shance's eyes fall into a well of sadness.

"She's been missing for over a month. She was a huge part of our community here, and she ran the hardware store next door. Hannah was one of the friendliest people in town," he said with pain in his voice.

"I'm so sorry, Sheriff," Reese said.

"Please call me Shance." He stood still and studied the room and Reese.

With the pleasantries aside, Reese and Shance shared one common goal tonight: making sure Gina was going to be okay. She asked Shance to stay a bit longer, just to ensure both Gina and her were safe. Reese felt a bit of hesitancy inviting him to stay for a while, as the shop was still in a dilapidated state. She didn't want anyone to see the shop in such disarray, but she had no choice. She was already feeling defensive and possessive about her new home.

"Would you like a cup of tea?" Reese asked, trying to break the tension.

"I'm more of a black-coffee man, but I'll try it," Shance said hesitantly. "So, is that what this shop is going to be? A tea shop?" he asked as he stepped toward the counter near Reese.

Reese explained to Shance that this old shop was going to mainly be a teahouse with some other curiosities. "It'll be similar to an apothecary, but with a twist." Reese smiled to herself as she fumbled through some boxes behind the counter that held aromatic teas.

"What's the twist?" Shance questioned as he pulled a chair up to the counter.

"Obviously, my name is Reese, and the name of the shop will be Reese's Pieces. And before you say anything about the chocolate, no, it's not a chocolate factory. I'll be displaying a small gallery in the back." Reese motioned toward the rear of the shop, where the bright white walls glowed in the night.

Shance straightened in his chair as he watched Reese pull a few jars of tea leaves from the packed boxes. "Can I be candid with you, Miss Reese? I am not a fan of tea." He studied her as if he were unloading a confession to a priest.

Without a second thought, Reese fired right back at him. "Well, luckily for you, I've been known to convince those who don't partake to become obsessed with my teas," she said with a smirk, knowing exactly which tea to choose for him: a blue-elderberry milk tea.

Reese started the small kettle she had set up against the window and grabbed two cups. As they waited for the water to heat, she took in the sight of her first customer. Shance was a very attractive man, and Reese had a hard time keeping her eyes off his toned arms. She felt as if she had to shake herself out of the thoughts that started to creep into her brain.

The kettle began its opera solo, starting as a whisper that was soon to be a full-blown crescendo.

Saved by the bell.

She reached for the cups and placed one in front of Shance, then put the raw tea leaves into a small fabric sachet before dropping one into each cup. Reese turned to grab the kettle and poured the hot water over the tea. The room immediately filled with the sweet scent of elderberry and blueberry with a dash of vanilla.

Shance's eyes became wild as he took a deep breath. He was damn near leaning over the bar, appearing eager to see if her tea tasted like it smelled. Shance finally complimented the scent that made its way into the entire shop.

"Oh, just wait. It gets way better." Reese smiled as she turned to grab the sweet cream to add to the steaming cups. She added the sweet cream and a few edible lavender petals for a warm aroma, then pushed a cup to Shance.

Shance took the warm cup in his hand and inhaled the first sip. After a moment's hesitation, Shance nearly downed the entire cup before Reese could sip hers. Reese smiled and held her cup with both hands, enjoying the heat against her chilled skin.

"That was a damn good cup of tea," Shance said. "I'll have to come back for more." He looked at Gina sleeping peacefully on the couch. "Well, Miss Reese, I hate to cut this short, but I should get going." He stood from his chair. "I'll stop by to check on Miss Gina here"—he motioned to Gina—"and, of course, to have more of that tea." A smile cracked across his face.

Shance and Reese said their brief goodbyes. Reese swiftly locked the door behind Shance and began to pull the old sheer curtains across the window before looking at Gina. What was she getting herself into? It wasn't her intention to have her on the couch, but Reese knew Gina would be better off on her couch than taken who knows where.

Reese took a deep breath, trying to keep her thoughts from going dark, and her eyes met Hannah's picture on the counter. Reese reached for the flyer to put on her community corkboard.

Seems like the right thing to do, Reese thought as she looked at the woman. Her heart sank again as she tacked Hannah's picture onto the board. Reese hoped they would find her. If it were her, she wouldn't want her family or friends to have to worry about where she was or if she was alive.

Four

*Obsession unravels like a tightly wound strand
of ribbon, each loop drawing tighter around my
fixation on her. It starts innocently: a casual glance
that lingers, a stroll through town, passing her shop.
It becomes habitual. Soon every detail is cataloged,
every movement monitored. Thoughts spiral into a
web of desire and control, where boundaries blur and
lines are crossed in the name of affection. Rationality
fades against the backdrop of all-consuming need,
a painting of love and possession merging into a
singular haunting silhouette. In the grip of such
obsession, the world shrinks into her, and everything
else fades into obscurity, becoming lost in the shadow
of an overwhelming desire to be hers.*

HE LOOKED AT THE FLYER IN THE FRONT SEAT, THE same flyer he'd stolen from one of the many businesses in Blue Sky. Her face was plastered around town. His fingers traced the cheek of the woman in the picture. Her skin was smooth, but not as smooth as Reese's, he wagered.

He needed Reese more than anything in this world. His hunger for her had grown each day since he saw her first painting in a gallery in Denver, and he would've had her if not for the stupid bitch.

She took her from me tonight, he fumed. He punched the steering wheel of his darkened truck, then took a deep breath. *I will get her. There's no need to be angry. I will have her.*

But how would he do it? He had to clean up his other mess first, he reminded himself. He needed to burn the clothing he wore that night, the same clothing that smelled like her: the woman from before, the woman from the poster. Hannah. They'd find her soon. Her skin was cold now, and her eyes no longer had the shine they'd had before. She was dead. He'd killed her, and he reminisced about how he'd done it. Choking her small dainty neck as she tried to escape, he'd felt every bit of life leave her body. He'd felt the warmth, her soul, leaving her body.

Although he knew the cops would figure out she'd been choked, he knew they wouldn't find him. He'd been masked and gloved when he took her life. But nevertheless, he had wanted everyone to know Hannah was taken by him, and him alone. He wanted his signature known. The chilling signature was a crimson ribbon tied tightly around Hannah's neck, a sinister mark of his twisted handiwork, a page he'd taken from Reese's creative flair. He knew that Hannah had been claimed as his, forever.

He'd loved every minute of swallowing her whole, of her faltering to him. He got off on her death. He pleasured himself to the thought of her finally succumbing to him.

He hadn't known taking the life of another person could be so satisfying, nearly intoxicating. He half hoped he could share that pleasure with someone. Well, not just *anyone*. Reese.

He wanted her, every part of her. He wanted to know what every inch of her creamy skin felt like. Wondering how she felt was what had driven him to kill Hannah. His hunger for Reese was insatiable. Reese was like an itch he couldn't scratch, so out of reach. It was starting to drive him mad. But still, he wanted so badly to tear her apart.

She was his obsession, an obsession he wanted to nurture. To nurture such a fire would surely grow it into a beautiful dark story of passion. No matter what happened, she was—and would always be—his. She just needed to know she was his. Forever.

He had followed Gina, Reese, and that asshole of a sheriff to Reese's shop. He knew she'd bought that building on the main street. Not a lot of people had known about it before Reese had shown up, but he did. He knew everything about her. Nevertheless, he'd never liked that building; everything from the windows to the peeling paint disgusted him.

He watched them go inside, Gina held in the sheriff's arms. If it were Reese in his arms, he would have killed that sheriff right on the spot for touching his beautiful prey. He stayed in his truck outside the building, keeping enough distance that the sheriff and Reese wouldn't see him. He watched through the window as Reese covered Gina with a blanket. Gina didn't deserve any of the attention she was getting from Reese, nor did the sheriff. Jealousy started to creep up on him again.

As he stared through the darkness, the sheriff exited the shop, taking one last look at Reese.

Fucking asshole, he thought. He wasn't going to have her.

"I will have her for my own. Just keep walking, Sheriff," he mumbled to himself in his truck as he slid lower in his seat, making sure not to alarm the lawman.

After the sheriff left, his gaze lingered on the shop, its warm light illuminating the main street. He had an urge to go inside and kiss Reese, to pin her against the wall and have his way with her. He had to resist—well, for a while. He couldn't muzzle his thirst for her forever.

He watched as Reese made her way to the top floor of her new place. Just looking through the large shop window, he couldn't see where her bedroom was. He decided to be a little riskier and get out of his truck.

Leaving his truck parked on the street, he made his way to the back of the shop through the small alleyway between the old buildings. The light upstairs flipped on, and he stalked his way to a dark part of the alleyway, looking straight up into her bedroom.

Her car was parked around the back. It was packed with household items, clothing in boxes, and everything she would need to start her new life.

He ran his fingers across the shiny car door and tested to see if she was stupid enough to leave it unlocked. Damn, it was locked. He peered inside, finding one of her paintings face up.

The painting was of pale feminine hands tied behind the woman's back with a ribbon. Maybe little Miss Reese wasn't as innocent as he thought; she had a dark side that was almost as dark as his. He was intrigued. His mind started to race with thoughts of tying Reese up. No woman would paint such a thing unless she wanted to be tied up herself, right? He needed to get that painting. He felt it was the perfect memento of hers that he could collect.

His impulse grew as he stared into Reese's car. He reached down to find a rock to break the window. He gripped the rock tightly, almost imprinting the sharp edges into his hand. Raising it above his head, he moved to shatter the window, but a dog's deep familiar bark broke the night's silence. The eruption of noise caused Reese's outside light to flip on.

Damn it, that fucking dog, he thought. Ducking away from the light, he hid in the shadows, holding completely still. Reese's shadow grew in the night, and then she peeked her head out of the rear window, pulling the white curtains to the side. Reese stood there for a moment, and his heart slowed to a near murmur. She stepped away into her apartment, her shadow fading from the window, and the lights flicked back off.

His heart finally came to a normal rhythmic beat, and his breathing slowed.

That was too close. She can't see me like this. His thoughts became clear. *I have to know her. I have to get close to her. I have to get her to trust me, otherwise someone will take her from me, and I can't let that happen. I'll do anything to have her. She's perfectly dark, like me.*

Something almost blissful started to grow inside his chest.

He gripped the rock in his hand, and his eyes flashed to the dog. It was fenced in the hardware store's alley, the same hardware store Hannah had owned. Thinking of Hannah again as part of the earth now, he smiled. His attention flashed to the dog, which was still staring into him, the same dog that had just interrupted him from getting that painting. Subconsciously, he rubbed his leg where a vicious bite still plagued his memory. Rage overtook him, and his grip on the rock tightened, his knuckles turning bright white, losing all blood flow. He almost let the anger take control, but he breathed in slow, and that blissful feeling came back to him. He dropped the rock and flipped the dog off as he got up from his kneeling position.

"Fuck you, dog," he whispered intently. "You're not worth my time. I have something better to hunt."

He'd thought of killing that dog more than once, but he knew he couldn't do it. He liked dogs more than people sometimes.

Dogs might bite, but they can never hurt you like a human can.

Even though he wasn't going to hurt the dog, he had to do something. This dog would bark again and alert Reese if he didn't take action. He turned to face the gate that held the dog in its small pitiful yard. Without thought, he unlocked the gate and walked into the night, knowing he had let the dog loose in town. He stalked away, getting lost in his thoughts of Reese, thinking of how beautiful she was and how much he wanted to be with her.

Soon. He would have her soon.

After he climbed into his truck, he looked back to see the dog moving cautiously from the alley. Its fur shined in the moonlight as it lifted its nose to a familiar but withering smell, and then it took off in the direction of the woods.

Five

THE NEXT FEW MORNINGS STARTED WITH A DAY-
dream of a modern take on an apothecary. Reese's ideas of
a huge open shop with warm light pouring in filled up her
heart. She had the idea of keeping the white-framed windows from the 1800s but adding small planter boxes on
the outside. As well as keeping all of the old Soda Fountain
shelving, she would add a rustic layer of patina to the metal
embellishments that were on each corner. She wanted to
add a thin layer of gray paint to the shelves to breathe new
life into them while not suffocating the history written into
the shelves. She reflected on this sentiment, breathing new
life into herself as well. She was ready for her new beginning.

Although her journey in Blue Sky had just begun, she
felt as if time was passing in the blink of an eye. Reese spent
most of her energy detail cleaning, getting every bit of must
and dust out of her shop. She had found the need to tape
brown parchment paper over the windows, leaving the outside town wondering what was going on inside. The sound
of hammers, drills, playful music, and some of Reese's off-

tune singing slithered out from the old building into the main street.

The street outside of Reese's Pieces was booming with talk of a newcomer who'd happened to arrive at the same time a woman had gone missing. The odd mixture of the two happenings seemed to almost divide and also intrigue the town. Reese didn't need to market the opening of her store, except maybe handing out a few flyers. She was lucky enough to live in such a small town that her business was going to attract attention; whether that attention was positive or negative was still up to the locals.

To Reese's surprise, Gina had recovered almost bafflingly well. It had only taken her a few days to be back to herself. Still, the scene at the bar shook Reese. Gina had gotten on with her life in Blue Sky, including helping Reese with her shop, getting it ready to open. Gina had cut ties with her date from the bar, which was the only decision she had made that Reese agreed with.

As Reese began to think of Gina's life, she had to remind herself that she couldn't get wrapped up in her promiscuous lifestyle. Reese had to concentrate on starting her new endeavor at Reese's Pieces. The shop finally had some soul put back into its shelves and was starting to look like an actual shop and not a ghostly mess covered in years of grime.

As Reese finished the final touches inside, she needed to start thinking of the presentation of the outside of her shop. Just like humans, the outside would always be judged before the inside. Reese had decided she needed a pop of color and a refreshing fragrance to welcome her patrons in. With that said, it was an excuse to explore the neighboring town, Zircon. Reese had found that Zircon had every-thing Blue Sky didn't, including a florist, big box-stores, home-improvement shops, and some hip breweries as well. Zircon was damn near a city compared to Blue Sky.

Reese had just finished planting lavender in one of the planter boxes next to the entrance of her shop and was starting on the other when there was a quick flash of light. She instinctively looked around, thinking of the old flash bulbs from retro cameras. Reese saw no one around, just a passing truck. The flash was probably from the passing truck's window reflecting on the dense shiny glass from the old downtown buildings. A shiny square-bodied black truck was parked down the street, and something about it reminded her she was in a small town. *There are more trucks than people here*, she thought as she turned back to the planters.

Her fingers were deep in the moist dark soil when a shadow fell over her, causing the warm sun to fade from her back. The light vanishing made Reese turn to the person behind her. The sheriff stood there, this time in his dark uniform and pristine white cowboy hat. Shance's uniform looked pressed and well taken care of. He nodded to Reese, and she stood to face him.

"Afternoon, Reese." Shance tipped his hat, his blue eyes gleaming between the wide brim of his hat and his nearly black shades.

That was something she'd have to get used to. *His eyes could cast a spell on any willing woman*, she thought.

"I wanted to stop by and let you know of some news around town." Shance took his sunglasses off. "The miss-ing woman, Hannah . . ." He seemed to be choosing his words carefully. "She was found a few miles north." Shance's eyes went dull. "It appears she was murdered, and even worse . . ." He stopped, choking back pain. "She was strangled."

Reese was shocked. She could see the hurt in his eyes. *He knew her*, she thought. Reese didn't know what to say. The only thing she could do was say sorry and console Shance.

"Thank you, Reese, but I do need to ask you some questions. Do you mind if we go into the shop?" he asked.

Reese couldn't read him. "Not at all. Please come in."

She walked to the shop door and held it for Shance. Before Shance entered the shop, Reese's thoughts began to swirl. *Do they think I did it? Why would he need to ask me questions?*

Shance stepped inside. "There's been some talk about your shop in town, and you showed up right after she disappeared." He adjusted his posture and tucked his fingers between his chest plate and his uniform, drawing Reese's eyes to his well-built chest. Shance's gaze shifted. Reese's eyes followed, and she realized he was looking at Hannah's picture tacked to the corkboard.

"Oh, wow," Reese said. "Well, I'm an open book. You can ask me anything you need to."

Reese sat at the counter and motioned for Shance to take a seat beside her. Shance sat, his posture still rigid. It made Reese wonder how uncomfortable the forty- or fifty-pound bulletproof vest was. It looked horrifying to wear.

Shance removed his pristine white hat and placed it neatly on the counter. "Do you mind if I take some notes?" he said, pulling his small notepad and pen from his vest pocket, the same small booklet he'd had the night they met.

Reese nodded. Although she had nothing to hide, she still couldn't help but feel uneasy about this.

"I know you just got here, but I'm asking everyone around if they've seen or heard anything from anyone. Hannah was loved by almost everyone in the town." It felt as if his eyes were penetrating Reese's mind.

Those beautiful seafoam-blue eyes, she thought.

Reese had to shake herself from his eyes. She'd been blindsided by the tone of his question, and she thought she was a suspect, probably based on what the other folks had said. "I'll be honest, Sheriff, I really don't know anyone but those I met at the bar the other night, you, and Gina. And I haven't heard anything from anyone."

"I understand. There are parts of my job that I don't like, and this is one part I hate asking." His words were dry. "But may I ask where you were a month ago, on the fourth?" Shance stared emotionlessly at her, his pen poised to write any detail that may come to mind.

"Oh, I was in Denver, preparing for this move. I was with my mom. I was in Denver until the tenth of this month." She looked to Shance with doe eyes. "You don't suspect me, do you?"

"Like I said, there are parts of my job I don't necessarily like, but I have to make sure I'm doing Hannah justice by finding out who is responsible for her . . ." He swallowed. "Death."

"I get it, Sheriff. I understand that this town is already talking about the new person on the block, and pointing fingers, from the sounds of it, but I can assure you that I wasn't even close to Blue Sky until the tenth. I can even give you my mother's information." Reese mirrored Shance, keeping her emotions tucked securely away. This was not the introduction she wanted to have with the town sheriff. Reese writhed, thinking of how she must appear to the locals. *They must think I'm a monster.*

"Thank you, Reese. I appreciate your honesty." Shance seemed to gaze straight through her. "And thank you for your time." He put the notepad and pen back into his pocket.

Shance was reaching for his hat when Reese cut the strange silence. "I'm sorry I can't be of more help, but you said she lived next door. Did she have a dog?"

Shance looked up at Reese with bold eyes. "Why?"

"I heard howling, barking, and damn near growling the other night," Reese explained.

Promptly, Shance took his notepad and pen back out. He asked on which night this had occurred and if there were any other details Reese remembered. Reese explained that the howling was on the night they had brought Gina to her shop. She didn't know what other "details" Shance was referring to, but she couldn't recall anything else from that night besides how quiet Blue Sky was compared to the city.

"Hannah did have a dog, Mr. Jingles. He's actually at the station now," Shance stated blankly, thinking about the poor canine that alerted local hunters to Hannah. The sight of seeing the canine curled into Hannah's cold body still shook him.

He quickly changed the subject, complimented the shop, and put his notepad and pen back into his chest pocket. He then made his way toward the shop entrance in one fluid movement. It was almost catlike, but not like a typical house cat. Shance was large and almost deadly silent in his motion—the same motion you would see in a panther stalking its prey. Before Reese let Shance slink off into Blue Sky, she handed him a flyer to her grand opening.

Shance nodded, taking the flyer and reaching for the shop door. His brooding light eyes were a storm. He held his emotions back so well, but Reese knew if she just tapped the glass, he would break free of his misery. Oh, how she wanted to shatter that glass, to let him escape and be himself. He was so closed off.

Before Shance could open the door, the bell on top rang, and Gina burst in without seeing the sheriff, her hands wrapped around a cardboard box.

"Oh, hey, Sheriff." Gina looked Shance up and down, practically drooling.

"Hello, Gina," Shance stated blankly as he turned to the door. "You guys be safe, and if you think of anything else, please give me a call." He closed the shop door behind him.

Gina shrugged him off. "He's uptight. You can do much better than him, Reese."

"I guess they found Hannah," Reese said before Gina could deduce anything else.

"Oh, yeah. I heard she was found tied up in the woods," Gina said. "Worst of all, they said her dog found her." She set the box down.

Those words sent Reese reeling, and her heart sank. She felt her world crumble, little did she know, the information she had just given Shance paint him a better picture of the timing of Hannah's death. "Holy shit." Reese sat, her lungs deflating in a large sigh.

"'Holy shit' is right," Gina said while unpacking new coffee cups from the box. "Sheriff sure looked like a ghost had walked into the room. Why was he here?" Her eager questions stung the air.

"He came here to question me," Reese explained with a heavy heart. Feeling the full weight of what had just happened, she added, "I think the town is pointing fingers in my direction."

"Of course they are. It's always something with these people. I swear this town just eats up gossip like it's a high school teenager," Gina said with a laugh in her voice, oblivious to Reese's somber attitude.

"Well, the sheriff doesn't seem convinced I'm not the murderer, that's for sure." Reese lowered her head into her hands, her wavy brown hair falling around her face. The pure melancholy tone of the day wrapped its fingers around her throat, gripping her. The air drifted away from her, her mind going dark. Like years before, Gina brought her back to the bright present.

Gina stopping unpacking and sat next to Reese. She tucked Reese's hair away from her face and started tracing shapes on her back, comforting her. "Reese, don't let the townies make you into a bad guy. You weren't even here when she disappeared. All they're doing is trying to make sense of something horrible. Besides, they said she was strangled. You don't look like the strangling type."

Reese caught herself smirking at Gina's logic. "Oh, really? What type am I?"

"You seem like the stabbing type for sure," Gina said, causing the shop to fill with both women's laughter.

Six

THERE WAS ONLY ONE DAY BEFORE THE GRAND opening. Reese had sent out a blast in the local paper and had handed out flyers. Blue Sky's locals had been skeptical at first, but Reese was now the talk of the town. Most of the residents were looking—seeming curious and border-line nosy—in Reese's direction, half suspecting Reese was a person of interest in Hannah's murder. Reese's grand opening party was going to be the highlight of the town's local gossip. Gina had heard from several locals that they were coming just to see what Reese was like. So Reese tried to spin her spell of a welcoming atmosphere. At her core, she was cynical at times, but she was going to be downright welcoming to her patrons tomorrow night. More than any-thing, Reese wanted to continue her adventure in Blue Sky, Colorado, so she saw it as imperative to get on good terms with most, if not all, of the locals.

There had been whispers in town that Reese had been talking to Hannah's family about creating a piece in honor of Hannah, which was to debut at the opening. Reese didn't want that news to circulate, but seeing as they were in a small town, everyone knew everything. Assuming there was a profit, Reese had decided that all proceeds from the opening night were going to be donated to help Hannah's family have a proper burial for her, as well as starting a college fund for Hannah's son, whom she'd left behind. To Reese's surprise, her talking to Hannah's family had divided the town. Nearly half the town had already decided she was Hannah's killer. That half of town thought Reese was mocking the family by helping them. The sane half was impressed with Reese's willingness to help the family, who were very dependent on the hardware sales to make a living in Blue Sky.

Still, Reese couldn't understand why the town thought she had killed such a beautiful woman who, until that flyer hit her windshield, she hadn't even known existed. She decided it was best to remain confused when it came to Blue Sky politics. She wasn't going to stir the pot. Well, she might stir it a little.

The town was right about Reese displaying a new painting, but little did they know the newest piece was of the beautiful Hannah herself. The painting was one of her best, and she thought it captured Hannah's beauty just right. Reese had made sure her pale pink lips were just as real as they would have been. The glimmer in Hannah's eyes was hard to replicate, but only the family would be able to tell Reese any different.

Reese wanted to ensure that Blue Sky was going to be her forever home, and she wanted to make sure her community was strong together. But she was slightly fearful that the locals might come at her with torches and pitchforks when they saw the painting. What is art unless it moves you, right? Still, Reese was more than willing to hand over her profits for her community, so maybe that spoke volumes to some.

Part of Reese wanted to know Hannah. From the sounds of it, she would have gotten along with her. Reese had learned that Hannah hadn't been born here, but she had convinced her entire family to follow her up the mountain to live a simple life. Would the family stay in Blue Sky? Only time would tell.

Reese's shop had gotten a lot of attention from the locals in the last week, so much so that the brown paper on the windows was now more of a deterrent for nosy townspeople than a way to hide the final product before her grand opening. Reese relished the time she'd had in the dark shop, but it was time to rip the metaphorical Band-Aid off.

As Reese started ripping off the paper that covered the shop windows, the warmth of the sun began heating her shop almost instantly. She tore the stale brown paper from the door, and as she did, her eyes met a rust-colored envelope taped to the outside.

The sun once again slithered into the shop as she ripped the paper farther down. Reese thought the sun had warmed her skin—or was it the eyes of the sheriff, who appeared to be walking toward the shop? He tipped his hat to her as he stepped closer. Reese unlocked the door with the heavy beaded skeleton key that hung in the knob. Reese opened the door to let the cool mountain air in. No matter how warm the sun was, the air always seemed to be carrying the sharpness of winter in every breath.

As the sheriff stepped closer, he removed the envelope taped to the door and handed it to Reese.

Reese grabbed the envelope from him, slightly brushing his large hand. "Hey there, Sheriff. What brings you over?" she questioned. She stepped to the side of the doorway, fidgeting with the smooth crimson paper in her hand. The envelope was thick and seemed like a custom size, not quite something you would get at the grocery store.

"I'm just checking in on you and Gina." He was holding a cup of what Reese presumed to be strong black coffee, and she decided that he seemed like the type that needed coffee to rise from the depths of the sleep that he so sporadically received. For a fleeting moment, Reese imagined what he must be like in the morning—tired, rolling out of bed to shower. Her thoughts trailed to water running over his muscular arms, and she had to stop right there. Thinking about Shance like that was surely showing on her now-blushing face.

"We're holding up all right." Reese pulled her thoughts away from Shance. Still, she had to pinch herself, and she even debated intentionally giving herself a paper cut with the envelope in her hand. Something about the stinging pain would knock her into the present. She had to keep herself grounded.

"Are you ready for your big opening?" Shance sipped his black coffee, peering over the thick steam that rushed out of the cup in his hand.

For a moment, Reese wished she were that cup of coffee. *His hands are strong too*, she thought. Reese had to damn near slap herself. Unintentionally, she started to fan herself with the envelope. There was a palpable friction between them. Reese knew what that tension was. It was an all-consuming attraction to a man who, by proxy, was cold-shouldered.

Smiling in an effort to conceal her string of thoughts, Reese said, "I'm ready, and I have a new painting I'm going to debut."

Shance just hummed and sipped his coffee. "I heard you've been speaking with Hannah's family. Word gets 'round quickly. I hope you're making the best decision for yourself, as well as for the family tonight."

His cold warning sent a shiver down her back. Or was it his seafoam eyes?

Reese had spent all her recent free time on the portrait of Hannah, and in her mind, this was a way to draw attention to her shop. As an artist, she was a bit afraid that this painting would be considered to be mocking the killer. Hannah's beautiful face would no longer be seen in this world except permanently on canvas. It would be displayed proudly. Reese was hesitant but also somewhat giddy, as she was generating the attention to her art that she'd always wanted. The talk of Hannah as a person has slowed to a halt in the last few days, so Reese's painting was another grand sign that Hannah should never be forgotten, and neither should her killer.

Reese stayed silent as she studied the man in front of her, his expression cold and masked. Shance was going to be a tough egg to crack.

"You know, you've been the talk of the town. There's a lot of attention being directed your way. I just wanted to make sure you're aware that there may still be a danger of someone willing to hurt women in this town. I'm not trying to scare you, Miss Reese," he said, his tone bringing out his slight drawl, "but I want to make sure that if you need anything or see anything suspicious, you give me a call."

"Of course, Sheriff. I'll keep my eyes and ears peeled." As Reese said that, a flash of light hit the corner of her eye. It looked like a flash from a camera. Reese directed her attention across the street, where she saw Michael, the Realtor, taking pictures of the hardware building next door. Reese waved to Michael as his eyes moved from the camera lens to Reese. Michael fumbled with his camera gear to wave back.

Shance looked over to Michael and nodded, tipping his hat in his direction. Shance looked back to Reese. "Well, I should let you prepare for your big day. G'day, Reese." Shance tilted his hat at her and stepped into the crisp morning air.

Reese shook off the odd feeling of Shance's warning. She knew that Hannah's killer was still out there and was starting to assume the sheriff had no idea who could have killed her. For a moment, Reese considered not revealing her painting. But despite the feeling of doom and gloom after that conversation, she wanted to see how the town would react. Maybe the killer would react stronger than the regular townsfolk.

Reese locked the shop door, then walked back to the gallery, still carrying the red envelope. She peered down at the envelope and fingered the seal holding it tight. Her gaze moved to the gallery wall, where the four-foot mural of Hannah lived. Reese stared into the painting, looking at Hannah's shining blond hair. She'd outdone herself with this piece As soon as she revealed it, she would cause the divide in the town to open into a metaphorical Grand Canyon. Her painting would surely be misunderstood.

The thought of the killer possibly looking at the painting made Reese's blood curdle. She started feeling ill. Maybe it was Shance's warning, or maybe it was the fact that Reese might not even have a business after the grand opening. Only Hannah's glimmering face could tell. Reese took one last look at the glossy painting before pulling the red curtain over Hannah's ivory skin.

Reese gathered herself, finally able to open the envelope and see what was inside. She pulled a smooth sheet of paper from the envelope, and her eyes met a black-and-white photograph. The photograph immediately made her heart stop. She couldn't breathe. The blood drained from her face.

The photo was of her planting the lavender. That flash she'd noticed *was* a camera.

Panic hit her heart as she fumbled with the envelope, trying to see if there was a note. In a moment, her whole world became small and insignificant. Reese felt lost, and the real danger of Shance's warning was true.

Seven

FINALLY, THE NIGHT HAD COME. REESE WAS GET-
ting ready for her big debut and making the final touches
in the shop when Gina walked in through the back entrance.

"Are you ready?" Gina asked as she grabbed a handheld
duster from atop the counter and started fiddling with it.

"It's now or never," Reese said with a hint of fear in her
voice. Seeing the photograph last night had made her more
wary about opening and showing the world *Hannah*. But
Reese, being the headstrong and determined type, told herself, *The show must go on*.

"Well, do you need me to do anything?" Gina started
idly dusting the detail work on the shelves.

"Just be here tonight, if you don't mind," Reese said,
knowing full well her eyes were going to be on the crowd
tonight.

"Of course," Gina said, still waving the duster around.

As Reese pulled Gina aside to go over the details of the
night, Gina brushed the duster across Reese's face, tickling
her nose. With a snicker, Gina made a slightly sexual joke

directed at Reese. "I was thinking about hiring a maid, but then I realized I already have enough dirty thoughts to clean up!" Reese pushed that aside and made Gina focus on the task at hand: getting this shop open and ready.

Reese had decided that because of the opening, each guest would get a complimentary cup of tea. Tonight's featured tea was a honey-lavender milk tea. Gina was in charge of handing out samples and ringing everything through the register.

Though Reese knew people would come and go throughout the evening, she would try to convince everyone to stay for the reveal of her new piece. Reese planned on talking with the patrons about her art and answer any questions they may have.

Reese walked to the gallery once more, the white walls so plain compared to her questionable art.

The town doesn't know what they've gotten themselves into, she thought.

Her art was not for the weakhearted; it was for those who could appreciate the human body in all forms. Each of the pieces showcased on the walls tonight was from her *Red* collection. The collection included Hannah's painting, which hung high on the wall with two spotlights on the deep red curtains. There was an ornate corded rope that Reese was to pull when the reveal would happen. Reese took one last look at her gallery. Each painting had its own story to tell, and Hannah's painting was going to be the talk of Blue Sky.

Reese had known as soon as she started the painting that what she was creating could be the end of her art career, or it could be the painting that set her apart from the others in the art scene. Blue Sky wasn't the place for an artist of her caliber though. That thought had crossed her mind more than once. Blue Sky was the last place for an artist like Reese, and she started questioning her decision to move there.

If the town was already thinking she could have killed Hannah, this painting might play into their suspicions. But Reese had nothing to hide, and if the town wanted to shun her for bringing more attention to Blue Sky and its townspeople, maybe she was wrong in creating *Hannah*. Reese shook herself out of her negative thoughts, then took a deep breath and walked into her shop, looking everything over once more before getting herself ready for her opening night.

Half an hour before the grand opening was supposed to start, the bell on the shop door rang. The first patrons of the opening started coming in, and before Reese knew it, more townspeople were flooding into the shop. She floated around the shop floor speaking with almost everyone, and it reminded her of why she'd moved here: the simple life.

The shop was filled with most of the town, it seemed, and everyone was speaking among themselves. Just as Reese was thinking about making her way to the gallery to reveal *Hannah*, Shance entered the shop. He was wearing a black cowboy hat and smirked at Reese from across the room. Reese's body heated up just from his smile. That was her cue, it was now or never to show her new piece to the town.

She grabbed a glass and a spoon and made her way to the gallery, where some people had already gathered, anticipating the reveal. Reese stood next to the tassel rope, where she could see the entire room. The guests' eyes fixated on her, and her face started to heat up from the attention. Bubbles of nervousness rose in her chest, her heart galloping. She was scared to do what she'd set out to do and feared causing a ripple that would turn into a wave in this small town. A lump formed in her throat as she thought of doing so.

She swallowed and attempted to get her bearings before she held the glass above her head and clinked it with the silver spoon. The room fell dead silent. Reese smiled, pushing her nervousness down into her chest.

"Good evening, Blue Sky. I'm so glad everyone here made it tonight, and thank you for welcoming me so warmly. As some of you know, I moved to Blue Sky about a month ago. Within that time, I had profound inspiration, the type of inspiration that could only be reflected on a canvas. With that said, please allow me to introduce *Hannah*."

Reese pulled the rope quickly, revealing Hannah's portrait, her blond hair glistening with gold highlights, her blue eyes as deep as a high alpine lake. There were a few gasps, and then the room fell completely silent for a moment. Reese could tell the townies' hearts were heavy. Just as she started thinking that maybe this was a bad idea, someone started clapping from the back of the room. Reese's eyes snapped to the back, where Shance was standing, clapping for her. Shance started the town up in a roar; a few whistles and a symphony of clapping surrounded her. A weight lifted as she stepped back into the crowd.

Reese's heart started to move back to its comfortable spot in her chest. The lump in her throat felt a bit smaller as she took in some air, finally able to breathe. As she moved through the crowd, she heard whispers—some of applause, some of disgust. As Reese had predicted, the town was torn.

"That was a bold move," a familiar smooth voice said from behind her. Shance made his way through the patrons, who were shuffling toward the gallery. "Bold moves like that can get you in trouble 'round here," he said as he reached her.

Reese had a hard time keeping her mind on the now-growing crowd; the only thing that mattered right now was Shance and his ocean eyes. "Someone has to make some waves around here." Reese curved her mouth upward to see the reaction from Shance—the reaction she'd wanted to see since the moment she first met him. He smiled, revealing delicate crow's-feet barely peeking out from both corners of his beautiful eyes. Reese debated showing him the photograph, but she decided tonight was her night.

"Goddamn, Reese, you sure are making waves. A damn near hurricane." His smile faded slowly. "But you have to understand, I'm concerned you're going to attract the wrong attention. Hannah's killer is still out there. What if they're here tonight?" His tone quickly changed from borderline flirting to serious.

Reese's smile faded. He'd made a valid point—a point she had already considered and dismissed. The lump in her throat came back. She started wondering if the killer was in the crowd. What if she had spoken to the killer? Paranoia crept up on her; her eyes started darting around the room. The crowd seemed to linger as she tried to study each of the locals. Reese snapped back to Shance, who had been doing the same thing, scanning the crowd.

"Do you really think they could be here?" she questioned, bringing Shance's gaze to settle on her face. His eyes seemed to warm her from the inside; she felt herself falling deeply into his eyes when his smooth voice washed over her.

"There is always a possibility, especially if the killer is a local." His words felt icy running across her skin. A shiver ran down her side. Reese wasn't sure if the shiver was from his warning or from his smooth, low toned voice that seemed to envelope her. Reese was in trouble, in more ways than one. She felt herself beginning to fall for Shance, but also, she started questioning if she was safe in Blue Sky with a killer on the loose.

Eight

*Obsession is the silent storm that clouds my
every thought, twisting like a ribbon around my
mind, pulling tighter with each passing day.
It clouds my every thought, weaving fantasies
into the fabric of reality, where your every move
becomes my universe.*

IT WAS FINALLY THE NIGHT HE HAD BEEN WAITING
for. He wanted to see Reese. His hunger for her had been
a constant on his mind, never ceasing, even in the quiet
night. He watched her every move any chance he had.
He had collected a number of photos over the last few
weeks. One of his favorites was of Reese planting flow-
ers outside her shop, her black pants barely dark enough
to hide her curves.

Even thinking about it, he couldn't help but feel a
surge of longing for her. He wanted to walk right up to
her and kiss her against the doorway. He wanted to steal
her away and make sure she knew how much he admired
her. He wanted her to know how he felt about her and how

no matter how hard he tried to fight it, she was his world. There were so many other things he wanted to do with her, but he had to keep his urges and desires in line.

He was excited to see Reese, to hear her voice, to see her milk-chocolate curls and feel her honey-brown eyes strike him from across the room. Maybe he'd even be able to speak with her.

He made his way through town, parking his shiny black square-bodied Chevy truck a few blocks away. Still, that wasn't saying much; the main street was only a few blocks long. From where he parked, the warm lights of Reese's Pieces shined like a beacon, lighting up the darkened street. He stepped out into the chilled night air, the moon shining over his black cowboy hat. He walked with his hands in his pockets until he reached Reese's Pieces. It looked like the entire town was here. He smiled. This was perfect. He pushed his way through the entrance door.

When he entered the room, it seemed to erupt with warmth and a concert of conversations. A soft fragrant smell hit his nose, teasing him. Reese. He knew it was her he smelled.

His eyes panned across the room under his cowboy hat. Reese stood elegantly clutching a cup of tea, as did the rest of the folks. He was so close to her.

So close I can almost taste her, he thought.

He was greeted by Gina, goddammit. He despised Gina, and he wished he could kill her. Maybe he would when he had the chance.

Gina crooked a cold smile at him and handed him a cup of tea. "Welcome to Reese's Pieces. Here's a sample of Reese's tea." There was no enthusiasm in her voice.

Maybe because she's talking to me, he thought. He hoped so.

He took the tea and nodded at Gina. He stepped away from the awkward encounter, and as he did, Gina mumbled under her breath, "What a fucking dick."

His face warmed with anger, but he shrugged her off and stepped into the crowd, making sure to blend in with the other men who seemed to be bored with this opening night.

He made his way to the gallery, where he found the majority of the men ogling Reese's art. He looked at the paintings that covered the reflective white walls. Much of her art focused on the female body. He stood for a few moments, staring at the same painting he had seen in Reese's car, the painting of the woman with her hands tied with red ribbon. Even tonight he still loved the piece.

As he stared at the painting, a breeze of warm air danced behind him, and he turned to see what had caused the air to shift. Reese stood a few feet from him, her back turned, talking with Hannah's mother, who was here tonight. His heart sank. He wanted to be close to her, to hear her voice, to be the one she talked to about her art. All the art in the gallery had deep undertones, each painting of a woman, whether covered in oil or dancing underwater. He made his way through the gallery. Reaching the back of the room, he found a door to the second floor.

Before opening the door, he threw the shitty tea away, discarding it in a nearby trash can. He didn't care for tea, even if it was Reese's. He peeked into the gallery to see everyone involved in a heavy conversation either about how fucked-up Reese was or how much they thought she wasn't a good fit for Blue Sky. He creaked open the door and slinked inside, making sure no one had seen him. Letting out one sigh of relief, he turned around and locked the door behind him. He found a small hallway that led to the outside of the building and tall wooden stairs that led to Reese's apartment. He made his way up the stairs, noting almost every step had a god-awful squeak.

Damn old buildings in this town. He stepped to the inside of each raised step to find they no longer squeaked when he shifted his weight against the walls. *Good to know*, he thought.

Reaching the top of the staircase, he found two more doors: one that led to the bathroom on the second floor and one that led to Reese's room. He stepped inside.

After closing the door behind him, he turned to face the room and was greeted with warm lights hanging from the ceiling and a large bed covered in cream-colored sheets. Reese hadn't made her bed. Something inside him was a bit disappointed. He'd expected Reese to have a high level of cleanliness. He brushed his hands across the sheets, feeling every ripple of the wrinkled fabric. He could tell Reese slept on the side closest to the stained glass window. He hadn't seen her sleep before, and it made him think of her peaceful features falling adrift in the night. Half of him wondered if he could see her bed from the outside. Though, now that he thought about it, the colored glass would make it impossible to see her. He became disheartened.

Continuing to look around the room, he found a small vanity that looked to be where she would get ready for the day. He walked over to the vanity and found a picture of what appeared to be Reese and her mother smiling in front of an art gallery in a city. Opening the drawers on her vanity, he found her hairbrush nicely tucked inside. He picked up the brush and dragged his fingers across the soft bristles, and when he did, it wafted the smell of her lavender shampoo to his nose.

God, she smells delightful, he thought. He had the urge to hold on to this small piece of Reese; without another thought, he placed the brush in his jacket pocket.

He then made his way to the other side of the room, where he opened her dresser. Inside he found a plethora of brightly colored underwear. He was astonished at how bright the colors she chose to wear were; he'd half expected her to have all-black panties, just based on how dark her art was. Digging through the dainty undergarments, he found a single pair of black lace panties. He held them up, imagining Reese in the skanky underwear. His groin pulsed just from the thought of Reese in them. He had to have these. He quickly stuffed the panties into his pocket and shut the drawer.

Feeling like he had gotten a good idea of the layout of the room and had figured out a bit about Reese, he made his way back down the stairs. With one last look upstairs to make sure nothing was screaming that he had been there, he unlocked the door. He peered through the crack in the doorway. Reese was walking to the covered painting, and everyone seemed to follow her in the gallery. She clanked her glass in her hand, and as she did, he slipped through the door and made his way through the crowd to hear what she was saying.

She pulled the ornate rope, and with one look at the painting, his heart welled up with fear and anger. Hannah. *Goddammit*. Doubt filled his mind. Did she know? Was she taunting him? Right when he thought the town had stopped talking about Hannah, Reese had to pull a stunt like that. *Fuck*, he thought as he tried to keep himself together.

His hands moved to his pockets, where he felt the hairbrush and the silky underwear. He had to get out of there, but he didn't want to make his disgust for her painting so apparent. He slinked to the back of the crowd, taking one last look at her. Reese was standing there in her deep red dress, smiling at the crowd. Most people found the painting to be a glorious depiction of Hannah.

Little do they know she was just a casualty of Reese being here, he thought.

He stepped back into the shop, where a few people were gossiping about how they thought Reese had killed Hannah. He ignored their ignorance as he left her shop. Taking a deep breath of the cold mountain air, he felt his worry leave him. He knew he had to get back at Reese somehow, and one thought rumbled in his head: *I have to get the painting, and if I can't, I'll destroy it.*

"Reese, you have a lot to learn," he said as he stepped into his truck. "And I think I'm the only one who can teach you a thing or two." He smirked.

He sat in his truck for a few moments, looking toward the bright shop, watching people leave Reese's Pieces. He had another thing to do tonight, but his plan wouldn't work until everyone left and Reese was in bed.

Nine

REESE AWOKE AFTER THE LONG NIGHT TO THE SUN
poking through her window just like the days prior. As she
yawned and stretched her way awake, she remembered she
still had to open the shop. As she panicked in preparation
for her first official day of her shop being open, she realized
it was already eleven in the morning. She rushed downstairs
and through the gallery and quickly snapped on all the
shop lights. She ran to the shop door and unlocked it in
haste. No one was there. *Thank goodness*, she thought.

Just as she turned around, she noticed an empty space
on the gallery wall. Curious, but also half-awake, she
blinked a few times and realized one of her paintings was
missing. Her heart immediately sank in her chest.

She rushed over to the wall to find *Bound* was missing.
At first, her eyes flew around the room. Maybe it had fallen
off the wall or gotten misplaced. But sure enough, *Bound*
was missing. Her heart shifted in her chest as she looked
around the gallery to make sure nothing else was missing.
Reese let out a slight sigh of relief as she realized *Bound* was
the only painting missing from the white gallery walls. She

felt angry but also confused, as she hadn't known that any of her pieces had sold last night.

Still giving the missing piece the benefit of the doubt, Reese grabbed her phone and sent a quick message to see if Gina had sold anything last night. She waited for a response; time seemed to stand still as she waited. Soon she saw three little dots light up her phone's screen.

"I only sold a few dried teas and some stickers. I made notes on what I sold on the ledger," Gina's message read. Gina responded right away to Reese's message, which was shocking, as Reese had not thought Gina would be awake this early.

Fear hit Reese, She had to remain calm, as she couldn't see an art theft in such a small town; something like that she could see happening in Denver, but not here. As she started to become more devastated by the thought of her work being stolen, her shop bell rang.

Reese's eyes flashed over to the door, where she saw Cody, the bartender, standing in the entryway. Reese had a hard time keeping her face bright and smiling as she made her way to the shop.

"Hey, Cody, I didn't see you last night," Reese said, stepping into the shop.

"Hi. Um, did I wake you up?" Cody said, motioning to Reese's pajamas.

"Oh my god, I'm so sorry. I overslept," Reese said as she realized that her silk pajamas weren't appropriate for work. Reese quickly grabbed an apron and covered her petite figure behind the stiff fabric.

"Well, shit, I thought maybe you'd just worn that to entice me," Cody said in his deep voice. He stepped toward the counter and sat with a large squeak of the barstool and a thud of his palms against the bar top. Reese walked around him. She wanted to make a sarcastic comment about how he wasn't her type and his comment was a reflection of his misogynistic demeanor, but she bit her tongue and walked behind the counter to face him.

He leaned over the counter. "So, what does a man have to do to get a cup of tea? I heard from the entire town that you have some pretty interesting combinations." Cody sat at the bar top, staring at Reese as she continued to tie the apron around the front of her waist.

Reese couldn't hold her tongue any longer. "I was half expecting you to pull a page out of my book and help yourself to something behind the counter." As soon as the words slithered out of her mouth, she wanted to backtrack. *Goddammit, Reese. Keep your mouth shut*, she thought. Her mouth got her into trouble more often than not.

Without another word, Cody stood from his stool and walked behind the counter, just as Reese feared he would do. As he inched closer to Reese, she backed herself up against the counter. Just inches from her face, Cody reached right above Reese's head while staring blankly into her eyes. He smelled of sage and clove. Cody pulled a jar of loose-leaf tea from the shelf and studied it, then turned away as if nothing had just happened, as if he didn't know how good he smelled to Reese.

"Cinnamon and bergamot," Cody stated. "Sounds strong."

After starting the water, Reese grabbed a cup from behind the counter and set it in front of him with a tea sachet.

"So, what brings you in? A tea shop doesn't seem like your kind of scene," Reese said as she took the jar of tea from Cody's hands and opened the tea to pour it into the sachet.

"Well, if you want the truth, you intrigued me at the bar a while ago, and I wanted to see if you would want to grab a drink with me." He was very direct.

"Oh, um . . ." Reese started to think of excuses why she couldn't go out with him, and her heart started pounding. *This is so awkward*, she thought. "I'll be honest: I'm not quite ready to go out on a date just yet. I just moved here, and I'm still getting settled in."

Before anything else was said, Cody stood from his stool and made his way to the shop door. "Well, when you're ready, you know where to find me," he said as he nodded and swung the door open in one smooth movement.

Reese had a hard time comprehending what had just happened. She looked down to the dried tea leaves still sitting in the sachet. *Am I still sleeping, or did that really happen?* She thought as she looked at her pajamas again.

Realizing she hadn't even gotten ready for the day, she quickly unwrapped the apron from her waist and made her way through the gallery. Once again looking at the blank spot on the wall, she was reminded she needed to call Shance once she was dressed to be in public.

Reese trotted upstairs, quickly grabbed some jeans and a T-shirt, and fumbled through her vanity, finding her hairbrush was missing. *Great, I must have misplaced my brush*, she thought as she ran back downstairs, making sure not to miss any potential customers. Once she reached the shop floor, her gaze darted outside. *Speak of the devil.*

Shance was once again in uniform. His arms seemed bigger, or maybe the uniform contoured to his smooth defined strength. Either way, he looked damn good. Reese's face flushed.

Reese ran outside to flag Shance down. He was walking away from the post office, carrying a small bit of mail.

"Excuse me, Sheriff, can I talk with you?" Reese said as she realized she'd run outside without shoes on. *It's just one of those days.* Shance turned to Reese and nodded.

"I think I might have had a theft last night at some point, and I have something to show you," Reese said, trying to hide the fact her bare feet were freezing cold on the cement sidewalk.

Shance cocked his head. "Sure, I'll meet you inside in a second. Let me drop this stuff in the truck." He motioned back to his truck.

Reese stepped back inside and quickly found a pair of slippers from behind the counter and slipped them on. Reese walked back to the gallery to look at the blank space on the wall once more.

Shance stepped inside the shop. He quickly removed his hat and moved toward the gallery. As Shance entered the gallery, his eyes went straight to the empty space on the wall.

"What was here?" The myriad of questions began to flow from Shance.

"This was *Bound*; it was here last night." Reese carried on, "I doubled-checked with Gina to make sure she didn't sell it."

"When did you notice it was missing?" Shance prodded as he reached into his vest pocket, once again grabbing his handy notebook.

"This morning. When I came down it was missing. I looked around the shop and it's definitely not here." Reese started to feel panic in her words.

"You said it was here last night, correct? When was the last time you saw it?" Shance's eye fixated on Reese.

"I can't remember, I feel like I would have noticed it missing before going upstairs for the night." Reese mulled over details of last night after everyone left. "Gina was the last to leave, and she helped me clean up the shop. She even locked the doors for me."

Shance made a note that he needed to talk to Gina too. "Do you have any enemies you know of?"

Reese was taken aback and thought Shance was being sarcastic. She started to laugh. But when she peered at Shance, his stern look said it all. "No, I barely have enough time to make friends around here, let alone enemies."

"I have to ask these questions for our investigation, as you know. How much is the painting worth?" Shance asked.

"Well, it's priceless if you consider it's one of a kind. But as far as how much I'd sell the piece for, it was marked at $1,000," Reese said as she pointed to the title piece on the wall with the price listed below the description of the painting, which read, "Ask Your Lover."

Shance looked at the price tag and title. "I'm not an art critic, nor do I pretend to be, but what am I supposed to ask my lover if I'm looking at this painting?"

"It's best if you see the painting. Here, I have a few pictures." Reese turned to go back into the shop and grab her phone.

While looking down at her phone, Reese shuffled into the gallery, where she wandered to Shance's side. Gina's message was still on the screen, along with a plethora of new messages from her:

"I saw it last night when I was sweeping the gallery." "Did someone steal it?" "I know I locked the doors." "Check your doors!" The spiral of Gina's thoughts became apparent. "Are you okay?"

Reese messaged her back, sparing a few details, but assured her friend she was okay and talking to Shance.

"Who could have killed such a beautiful woman?" Shance asked out loud as he homed in on Hannah's painting.

"That's the question of the century," Reese said as she pulled up a photo of the painting that had been stolen.

Shance took Reese's phone and stared at the painting. "Can you send me these pictures? And do you have cameras in your gallery, by chance?" Shance asked.

"Of course I can send them. And I hadn't thought that I needed cameras in such a small town, but I guess that serves me right for thinking people are capable of being good," Reese said darkly.

"Not everyone is bad, Reese. But I do suggest that you cover your bases. You had almost the entire town in here last night. Did anything else go missing?"

"Well, my hairbrush, but I might have misplaced it in the shuffle of moving everything around," Reese said, shrugging off the possibility of her brush being missing. "I'm sure it'll turn up. If not, I'll buy another, no big deal. I just don't understand why someone would steal art."

"You know that Blue Sky is in the headlines; attracting a lot of attention from outsiders, there is a possibility that now you are in the town's headlines. Everyone has been talking about you, Ms. Reese, even before your painting of Hannah. Someone could have wanted the painting to say they were part of history." Shance's speculation began to form. "But this doesn't happen in Blue Sky." He hesitated. "Not before, anyway." His tone had shifted, making Reese think he was pointing the blame in her direction.

Reese stared at him blankly, his words stinging her. She remembered she had to show him the photo. This was surely going to shake him up, and his idea of Blue Sky being "safe."

Reese's heart sank, and that eerie feeling surrounded her again. She led Shance to the front of the shop, where she pulled the red envelope from a drawer behind the register and placed it in front of Shance.

Shance's curiosity piqued as he looked to Reese with his light eyes. He opened the envelope and immediately dropped it onto the counter, carefully examining the photo of Reese, prodding it with his pen, noting any blemishes on the glossy finish of the photo.

"When was this taken?" Shance questioned Reese urgently.

"A few days ago. Before I opened the shop." Reese sensed herself pulling away, retreating into the depths of her mind.

"Did you notice anything out of the ordinary that day?" Shance followed up.

"I thought there was a flash, but I blew it off to a truck passing by that reflected the sun." She sighed, feeling the shame that came with her ignorance after looking back.

"What kind of truck?" Shance continued to ask her questions.

"I am not sure. A dark-colored truck, old, like your patrol truck," she stated, lifting her chin to the truck parked outside.

Shance's eyes followed Reese's eyes. "Look, Ms. Reese, I am going to do my best to get to the bottom of this. Do you remember anything else?" he concluded as Reese shook her head.

Shance pushed off the bar top and placed the notepad in his vest pocket. "Well, give me a few minutes; I need to get this typed up," he said as he motioned toward the shop door.

"Thank you, Shance," Reese said as she followed him to the door. Shance, for a moment, turned back, looking at Reese. As he stood in the doorway, the threshold seemed to shrink just from the size of his broad shoulders. He put his cowboy hat back on and stepped outside to his truck.

Reese watched Shance as he furiously typed away on the onboard computer in his truck. At least she'd reported the crime and the photo; it made her feel a bit better. She knew now that one other person knew. Part of Reese was also thankful she'd been able to see Shance again, though something told her he wasn't interested in anything but helping his community. Shance was a good-looking man, and Reese was sure that if he had his way, he wouldn't be alone—but he did have that professional loner thing going on.

AS SHANCE TYPED UP A REPORT IN HIS TRUCK, HE knew the only reason he was in there was to catch his breath. There was something about Reese that made his blood boil—not with anger, but with passion. He had to collect himself. His focus narrowed.

Crimes like this didn't happen in Blue Sky. As soon as Reese had shown her face, though, the town had started attracting attention, and not the attention he wanted. The department wasn't any closer to solving the Hannah Franklin case. He'd heard that a reporter from Denver was about to publish an article that surely was to frame Blue Sky in a dark light the town didn't want.

These things don't happen in Blue Sky, he kept saying to himself, wondering if he was repeating the words to convince himself or others. He felt devastated that he no longer could say Blue Sky was safe; his heart sank a little. Shance had the oddest feeling that the drugging of Gina at the bar, the theft of Reese's painting, and the photograph were somehow connected. Even worse, Shance's gut told him that there was something more nefarious going on.

On the same train of thought, he started to think of who'd been at the bar and also at the opening night, which really didn't narrow down any suspects. Almost the entire town had been to Reese's opening, but not as many people had been at the bar that night.

Cody was always grumpy, never really personable. He had quite a long rap sheet with the Blue Sky Sheriff's Department, though all of Cody's crimes were mainly petty ones at the very least, like speeding through town or running red lights and stop signs. Even though Shance had never cared for Cody as a person, he couldn't picture him murdering someone. Cody hadn't been at the opening last night, but that still didn't rule him out as a suspect for the drugging.

Michael, the local Realtor, had been at the bar, and Shance even thought he'd seen him at Reese's opening night. Michael always kept up on his public appearance. He made friends with the local city council, and in fact, he attended every city council meeting. No matter how boring that may sound, Michael seemed to like hearing about upcoming projects, which, in turn, gave him the upper hand when selling buildings around town. Michael didn't really have any friends—well, outside of work, anyway. He didn't seem to mind the quietness of being a technical loner though.

Shance began to suspect Michael. He was a likely candidate, but he would have a lot to lose if he killed someone or even stole a painting. All of that seemed a little reckless for Michael, which was something he wasn't.

Gina had obviously been at the bar, incapacitated, and at the opening. Shance couldn't even begin to think Gina was smart enough to drug herself to throw the sheriff's department off her trail. But stealing a painting wasn't below her. Gina had also had run-ins with the sheriff—multiple times, in fact. She'd been caught stealing from the local grocery store several times, so much so that Gina had been banned from the store. She hadn't made the best decisions in her life, but once again, murdering someone was very far off from petty theft.

Gina's conquest, David, had been at the bar that night, Shance remembered. Shance didn't know too much about David, and he was the likely suspect of drugging Gina. When Shance had questioned him, he'd been more upset than anyone, mostly because he'd thought he and Gina really had a romantic thing going on. That night had ruined his chances with her, which could actually be a reason why he would steal a painting from Reese.

Shance didn't throw out the idea of Reese being the killer or even the thief. But how could she have taken a picture of herself?

It'd be a clever move to stage a theft from your own shop to throw off the police, Shance thought. But there was something off about that. Reese had told him exactly where she was the night Hannah was believed to have been kidnapped and murdered. Shance hadn't followed through with her alibi. He had to make sure speaking with witnesses was on the top of his priority list. Why was it so hard for him to believe Reese might be a killer?

There had been maybe five others in the crowd at the bar, all of whom had been at the opening.

Vickie and Jack were happily married and always with each other no matter the circumstance. The other person who stuck out to him was Devin.

Devin kept to himself and rarely spoke to other people. Shance considered Devin a shut-in, but he didn't interact with Devin too much; in fact, no one really had a lot of say about him, as he rarely made appearances in public. Shance

Suspected Devin was a part-time local. He had heard Devin owned a large property on the outside of town and frequently visited when not on business ventures. Devin was well off, from what Shance gathered.

As Shance continued to think of other townies who could have committed such a crime, he started to suspect everyone equally. Shance finished up gathering his thoughts and made his way back into the shop.

Reese was waiting near the counter when he walked back inside.

"All right, I have all the information in. I'm going to make sure this gets resolved as soon as I can." He tipped his hat once more. "I do, however, suggest you invest in some camera equipment for your shop." He remained professional and to the point.

"Okay, Sheriff, thank you so much for looking into this for me," Reese said with a wave of disappointment on her face. "I guess I'll have to keep my eyes on everyone and everything that isn't bolted down." Attitude leaked from her words.

Shance turned to the door. As he reached for the doorknob, an idea popped into his head. "You know, I may be able to swing by every so often to make sure nothing goes bump in the night," he said, looking at his truck parked outside.

"That would be amazing, but I don't want to put you out," Reese said, slinking toward him from behind the counter.

"Oh no, that wouldn't be the case. I'd rather know my town is safe, just as anyone else would," he said, turning back toward Reese, who was a few feet from him now.

"Well, thank you, Shance. You're too kind to me."

"I'll see you later, then," Shance said, opening the shop door to the warm sun.

Ten

TWO MONTHS AGO.

Hannah brushed her straight blond hair from her shoulders as she stepped into the real estate office in Blue Sky.

Michael greeted her with a smile. "Hannah, so good to see you. What brings you in?"

"Good morning. I swung by to see your smiling face, of course," Hannah stated as she came up to Michael for a side hug, the normal greeting between the two. "Actually, I was just looking into the old Soda Fountain space. Do you mind if we take a look at it? I'm thinking about expanding the hardware shop."

"Oh, definitely. Let me grab the keys real quick. But I have to say, I have a buyer from Denver who's interested in the property as well." Michael stepped behind the counter and unlocked a safe that held the keys for the current for-sale homes and businesses in Blue Sky.

"Oh, I heard. Small town, Michael," Hannah said, sarcasm dripping from her lips. "But I figured I'd see how much work this place would be and hopefully swoop it out from underneath them." She smirked.

Michael and Hannah headed out of the office, deep in small talk about the town. Michael suggested they walk to the Soda Fountain, as it was only a few blocks away. Hannah fired back at him with a blank stare, as if she was astonished someone would want to drive just a short distance.

When they made it to the Soda Fountain, Michael inserted the old skeleton key and pushed the squeaky door to the side for Hannah.

She could see the potential of the Soda Fountain already. The old bar top would have to be ripped out, but other than that, there wasn't much else that needed done to the space. Hannah walked through the back room and opened the door to see a rear entrance and stairs to a possible apartment. She stepped upstairs to see what the second floor held. She opened the bedroom door to be greeted by a huge stained glass window. The window painted the open space with small smudges of color. Hannah admittedly was blown away by how much light was inside the upstairs. After taking one last look, she made her way back down to Michael.

Michael was running his fingers across the dusty bar top, looking at the old shine underneath the dust, when Hannah walked to the front of the shop.

"So, tell me about this Denver buyer. Is there a chance I can snag this from them?" Hannah asked as she looked around the shop space more.

"All I know about the buyer is that she had some major luck in the art scene in Denver. She sold a collection of paintings to an art collector. At least, that's what I could gather online," Michael stated.

"So she has money to spend. But how successful can art really be? I mean, how much is art really worth?" Hannah inquired, mainly to herself. She smiled at Michael, who was wandering around the shop, somewhat in a daydream.

Hannah thanked Michael for showing her the Soda Fountain and said her goodbyes, giving him a kiss on the cheek.

She mulled over the idea for the next few days. She finally made a decision as she closed up the hardware store: Hannah wanted the space. She needed to make more room in her hardware store soon anyway, and her shelves were starting to look packed to the brim with odds and ends.

As she looked at the business card she'd snagged from Michael, her excitement was palpable. Hannah grabbed her purse and keys from the counter at the back of the hardware shop, already daydreaming about how she would open up the hardware store and convert the up-stairs into a two-bedroom home for herself and her son. Hannah petted Mr. Jingles, whose thick tail smacked the sides of her legs. Mr. Jingles had become a local celebrity with the townies. He was so popular that part of Hannah's profits was selling shirts with Mr. Jingles's face on them. Hannah petted Mr. Jingles one last time before looking at her shop, already envisioning the new hardware store.

Turning to the door, Hannah flipped off the lights to her shop. As she pulled the chain attached to her neon

Open sign, an arm wrapped around her waist and a hand covered her mouth. Already starting to feel lightheaded, Hannah screamed and kicked at the person holding her. The rag that covered her mouth smelled of strong chemicals that burned the inside of her nose. She was dragged back into the dark store and away from the windows.

Mr. Jingles ran to Hannah's side, where he growled and nipped at the dark figure that held Hannah tight. As Mr. Jingles bit into the assailant's leg, the shadowed figure kicked Mr. Jingles to the side. Mr. Jingles whimpered in pain as his head smashed into the ground from the person's heavy kick. With wary eyes, Mr. Jingles peered through the dark, growling as Hannah struggled against the assailant.

The canine barked as Hannah became weak, still trying to fight against the awful smell coming from the rag covering her mouth. Hannah's vision became blurry. She was struggling to fight the darkness closing in on her. In the darkness, among the dog's barks and wails for help, Hannah went limp. Her fingers loosened, dropping Michael's business card onto the ground.

Eleven

THE DAYS SEEMED TO BLEND TOGETHER. THE MORN-ings and evenings were feeling more like winter. Something Reese hadn't had a second thought about before moving to Blue Sky were the deep reds and purples of the sunsets. She was so used to the Front Range sunsets in Denver. Those colors were bright, but not as deep as the ones in Blue Sky. She made it a point to witness them every night before closing up shop.

Reese stood at the bar-top counter as she greeted a dapper gentleman who pushed open the entrance door. Reese helped the older man, whom she now knew as the florist from Zircon. Reese had proctored a deal to help each other's stores. It was this tight-knit community that made Reese feel safe and at home. The florist had agreed to trade plants for her store windows, adding to the atmosphere of the shop, and Reese had allowed him to take samples for his Zircon shop to add to gift baskets. Reese was astounded by how the plants had added such a personal feel to the shop. Each of the plants seemed to thrive, even just being in the direct sun for a few hours a day.

Reese met someone new almost every day. It was still astonishing to her, and her thoughts of Blue Sky being so small seemed to be fading quickly each day. The bells on the door rang again, and Shance stepped in with a furrowed brow.

"Good to see you, Sheriff," Reese said with delight in her tone. Realizing the curtains were covering the shop windows, she walked over to open them up for more light to dance inside the shop. "What brings you in today?" she questioned as she tucked each curtain into the curtain hooks.

"I have some news that you might want to hear," Shance said, taking a seat at the bar top, removing his hat along the way. He took a deep breath.

Reese sat next to Shance at the bar top. Something wasn't right by his demeanor. Reese could feel the weight of the conversation; it made her want to crawl out of her skin and run from the shop as fast as she could. The horrible feeling of trouble lurking behind the corner nearly swallowed her. But as afraid as Reese was, she sat eagerly waiting, her feet and hands tingling with suspense.

Shance took another deep breath. "I was speaking to Hannah's family, and some small details emerged." Shance carefully looked at Reese, studying her face. "Hannah was going to purchase this building before you." He paused, allowing Reese to comprehend how this must make her look.

"Wow, okay. Well, what happened? I didn't hear that there were more offers on this building when I put my bid in." It dawned on her that if she hadn't been considered a suspect before, now it looked even worse for her. That feeling of community and being safe suddenly dropped from her heart.

"Hannah didn't have time to put the bid in; she went missing after she toured the property with the Realtor," Shance confirmed, still looking at Reese, likely to see her reaction.

The town already suspected her of killing Hannah, and it seemed that Shance was starting to doubt Reese's innocence. The blood drained from her face, and she felt sick to her stomach. "I assure you, I can provide any detail of where I was when Hannah went missing," Reese said, swallowing the frog in her throat.

"I know. In fact, I spoke to your mom and the gallery you were at." His gaze lowered. "What I'm trying to say is that I don't think you had anything to do with Hannah's murder. This building could have been a motive to kill Hannah. We haven't found any other reason someone would want to hurt Hannah, and as the rightful owner of this building, I thought you should know," Shance blankly stated, still looking to Reese, who was reeling from the new information.

Reese swallowed again as fear crept up inside her. "Am I in danger, Shance?"

Shance grabbed Reese's hand and held it on the bar top. "There is a possibility." His words were heavy. "I want you to know the details as they unfold. I think whoever is responsible for Hannah's murder, Gina's drugging, and the picture are the same person. If not, they're related in some way. This seems to circle around you." Still holding Reese's hand, he said, "And like I said before, I will be stopping by every so often to check in."

Reese looked at Shance holding her hand. It gave her some comfort knowing that at least one person in town was looking out for her. She didn't move her hand but instead kept it securely tucked in his. As her thoughts began to swirl, she fixated on the fact that Shance had spoken to her mother. He must have heard about her past. There wasn't a day that went by without her mother checking in on her because of what had happened.

Just as Reese was starting to feel comfortable in Shance's hands, the bells on the shop door rang. Today was busy. Reese and Shance looked to the door and saw Gina.

Reese quickly slipped her hand out of his and greeted Gina with a smile and a hug. Gina smiled and squeezed Reese back, tucking Reese's hair behind her ear after the embrace.

Shance stood from the bar top and made his way to the shop door, pausing before leaving.

"Reese, I'll be back tonight. Let me know if you need anything," he said before making his way outside.

After the small bells on the door went silent, Gina and Reese sat quietly at the bar for a moment before Gina broke the silence with her accusing tone. "All right, give me the details." She swirled her fingers around Reese's palm. "How good is Sheriff in bed?"

Baffled and taken back by Gina's accusation, Reese pulled her hand from Gina's playful touch. "Gina! The sheriff and I were talking about Hannah's death." She sat back on the barstool, eyeing her.

"Oh, shit," Gina said in a soft tone. "Sorry, that definitely wasn't the vibe I was getting from the hand holding at the bar when I walked in." Her tone was short, almost tinged with jealousy, something Reese had never heard from her before.

Reese tilted her head at Gina, her eyes narrowing. Something told her to keep things light. "I can't say that I haven't thought about his arms around me," she admitted. Reese and Gina erupted in laughter together, as they always did when it came to talking about men. Gina seemed to get a kick out of having walked in on Shance and her holding hands. Just what Reese needed: more gossip around her and her shop.

Any publicity is good publicity, she told herself, but the logical side of her was fighting the urge to lash out and lock her doors for good, especially if this building was the target for the killer.

Twelve

THE SUN WENT DOWN SO QUICKLY TODAY, REESE thought as she started to clean the shop for the night. It seemed like the sunset tonight didn't have those same colors. Maybe it was Reese projecting onto the sky, but even the clouds seemed lifeless.

She locked the shop doors and grabbed the broom from the cleaning closet. She turned on some music and started sweeping the original creaking wood floors. While Reese cleaned, she noticed Shance's vehicle pull up across the street and shut the lights off. Reese wondered if he would stay outside, looking at the shop, or if he would come inside. She didn't know how to handle the situation. Why couldn't she get him out of her head? Part of her wanted him to come inside, but her other half wanted to steer clear of the drama in town. She wanted to lie low from the town's eyes and just run her business and be a good neighbor.

Reese finished wiping down the counters in the shop, and when she went to close the sheer curtains, she noticed Shance again. With the silver-blue moonlight hitting the shine of his black truck, the warm cab lights lit up the street below his truck. Something told her to invite Shance in. Reese made her way behind the counter and hung her apron up, then headed to her apartment above the shop. Reese decided if Shance was still outside after she showered, she would invite him in. A compromise with the devil on her shoulder.

As Reese showered, thoughts of Shance danced in her head. The idea of him as a Spartan in Rome felt right to Reese. He was a down-to-earth man, though with some antisocial and general avoidance tendencies sprinkled in, but there was nothing wrong with that in Reese's eyes, especially given that he was a sheriff. Reese could sense that Shance didn't want to overstep his boundaries, but she also knew there was some chemistry between them.

Reese stepped out of the shower and dried herself off. She braided her wet hair, which reminded her that she had to get a new brush. She dressed in black leggings and an oversize shirt. As she put on her slippers, she peered out the window to see Shance still sitting in his truck, the silhouette of his face being lit up by his phone; which echoed into the deep night.

Well, she thought, *I guess I'm calling my own bluff.* Panic hit her heart as the nervous butterflies in her stomach pushed her downstairs.

She passed the empty space on the wall. Her heart sank again. It was a dark reminder of how vulnerable her shop was. She had to carry on though; she had no other choice.

Reese made her way to the bar top, where she decided to make Shance a cup of tea for the cold mountain night.

Reese made a mix of Earl Grey, lemon, and sweet cream.

She clicked the lock on the shop door and pushed the door open. The breeze swirled around her. Winter was fast approaching, though it felt like summer had just blinked by. The cold night air smelled of wet leaves that had recently fallen to the ground.

Reese silently headed toward Shance's truck. As she reached the amber light pouring out from his cab, the scent of warm sandalwood hit her nose. *Shance.* She shook herself and lightly tapped on the window.

He jumped out of his skin for a flash of a second, then rolled down the window. "You scared the daylights out of me." Shance's slight drawl came out; he must've been reeling from being shaken out of his daze.

Reese laughed it off. "Sorry, I didn't mean to scare you. But if you'd been paying attention to the shop, you would have seen me make you some tea." She handed him the tea through the truck window.

Shance took the tea in his hands. "Thank you, but you know you didn't have to do that."

"Nonsense. You're out here in the cold, waiting for something that probably won't happen with a sheriff truck parked outside." The sarcastic words were her attempt at light flirty banter.

Shance shook his head and smirked. He got her sarcastic humor, which was a huge plus. He took a sip of the tea, and the earthy tones of the Earl Grey with the zest of the lemon seemed to wake him straight up.

"Wow, that tea is somethin' else," Shance stated, once again bringing out a slight twang in his voice. He took another swig.

Reese giggled. "Yeah, I thought you'd need some form of energy if you were going to be out here in the dark. I wouldn't want you falling asleep in your car." She was testing the waters. She hoped he would be open to the idea of coming inside the shop. *What the hell.* She gathered herself. "You know, you'd be more comfortable inside the shop." She stared as he mulled over the idea.

With one nod, Shance took another sip of the tea as if it were his liquid courage.

Shance rolled his window up and popped the door open.

"Oh my, I thought it would take more convincing," Reese said with a smile across her face.

Shance smirked at her and jumped out of his truck. "What can I say? That's some damn good Earl Grey."

Astonished that he knew his tea, Reese fired back, "You know your tea. Color me impressed."

Shance locked the truck. They turned to the shop, which seemed to light up the entire ghostly main street. As they walked to the shop, their conversation shifted to how beautiful the night was in Blue Sky. The night was something that most locals never cared to experience. The town was a literal ghost town at night; nothing was open, minus the bar, with its neon lights seemingly flashing throughout the dark street, no people or cars were in sight.

"I always forget how quiet it is here," Reese said, reaching for the shop door. Before she could pull it open, Shance jumped in front of her and held it open for her. "Thank you, sir." Reese stepped back inside the warm shop.

"You'll never get used to how quiet it is here. I haven't yet," Shance said as he turned to close the door behind him. "I'm sure you're used to city noises being in the forefront of everything all the time."

"Yeah, you're right. But there's something about Blue Sky's nights. They make me feel like I'm right at home but also very far away from reality at the same time." Reese got lost in her words.

Shance smiled at Reese and made his way to one of the couches in the shop. Reese followed and sat next to him.

"I hate to be too nosy," she said, "but I feel like I know so little about you, while at the same time you seem so familiar."

Shance took another sip of tea. "Well, what do you want to know? There isn't much to me. I'm not a Colorado celebrity like you."

"Well, not yet," Reese interjected. "When you solve Hannah's case, you'll forever be the small-town sheriff who solved a murder."

"Let's not talk about that right now. It's been taking up so much of my time that I don't want it to take this too."

Reese smiled, getting the hint. "Well then, what do I need to know about the badass Blue Sky sheriff?"

"I'm serious, there isn't much to me. I spend my time working, exercising, and fixing up the old house on the hill on Main."

"Oh, the one with the wraparound porch?" Reese lit up. "I love that house. How long have you been fixing it up?"

"My grandparents gave me the deed about ten years ago, but they left it in shambles. That house was enough to get me to move to Blue Sky."

"So, if you've only been here for ten years, where did you live before?" Reese inquired.

Shance hung his head low. "Denver."

"Oh, interesting. So I'm not the only city slicker around here, then."

Reese and Shance carried on the conversation about Denver and how crowded and unfriendly it had become in the last few years. They reminisced about how open the city used to be, and Reese told Shance how overdeveloped Denver had become and that the art scene was in shambles too.

"I have a show coming up soon that I have to go back for, and I'm not looking forward to being back in the city." Reese hung her head low.

She was testing Shance's reaction to hearing about her mom, trying to figure out how much he might've been told. Shance nodded and took the obvious bait.

"Your mom told me about your ex. What happened?"

"He was abusive. He beat me up, and Mom found me on the front lawn covered in blood, barely breathing. He's in prison now."

Reese was up-front and told him everything about her past. It was a downer to think about, and as she finished her story of her mom finding her, she ended on a head-strong note. "I'll never let anything like that happen to me again. I won't give power to losers like that." She glanced down to find she was fidgeting with her fingernails. Although the past was not there to hurt her, she still felt the sting. She looked up at Shance, who gave her a reassuring smile and quickly changed the subject.

Shance and Reese began to swap stories of their childhoods, finding they had more in common than they'd originally thought. They had eerily similar stories of places they'd been. Reese found out that Shance had been alone in Blue Sky since he'd moved in and hadn't found any of the townies desirable.

Shance was blunt. "You're so beautiful. I haven't really had the chance to tell you."

"I'm humbled. Thank you, Shance."

Before Reese could say anything else, Shance leaned in and kissed her. Reese could feel his raw desire for her and became weak just from his kiss. That tiny voice inside her head telling her not to kiss the sheriff faded to a murmur, then a whisper.

Reese kissed Shance back, running her hands through his soft dark hair. Shance moved closer so he could push a single strand of hair away from Reese's face. He moved his hands to her petite waist. Reese held both of her hands behind Shance's neck. Shance pushed Reese down into the soft couch; she instinctively wrapped her legs around his waist. His desire throbbed against her, and her body begged to know how he really felt.

Shance came up for a deep breath. "Is this okay?" He stared down at her.

Reese lifted herself to meet his kiss, her fingers gliding slowly through the thick, velvety strands of his dark hair, once more, savoring the warmth and softness as they intertwined. Showing she wanted him too, she pushed herself up, moving him back to a seated position. As she did, she slid into his lap, her legs still wrapped around his waist. She gave him a flirty amount of tongue, and he kissed her back, his tongue dancing with hers.

Shance's kisses were intoxicating. His fingers tracing the small of her back sent chills up her spine. Reese closed her eyes as his fingers danced through her hair. He pulled her head back, exposing her neck to him. He trailed kisses down her neck to her collarbone. Shivers rose along her arms, down her sides, and throughout her body.

Without warning, a flash illuminated her closed eyelids, and a shattering noise pierced the air. Shance and Reese stood within an instant. They peered through the sheer curtains to see hazard lights flashing in the night.

"Motherfucker!" Shance shouted as he pushed past Reese to swing the old shop door open. Reese ran after him, fully taking in the scene of an old pickup that had run right into Shance's truck. Shance ran to the pickup, the lights flashing and the engine hissing as if panting its last breath.

Shance pulled the door open to find Cody passed out and hunched against the wheel. A bottle of Jack fell from the cab as Shance unbuckled Cody and pulled him from the car. Cody moaned drunkenly as Shance yanked and pulled on him.

Soon the town came back to life as lights started turning on to see what had happened. The town started bustling as if it were broad daylight. Reese stepped back, letting Shance do his job, something Reese did not envy: dealing with onlookers and a now-belligerent Cody, who was yelling about the flashes of light. He needed to be restrained by a sheriff's deputy to be put into the back of his patrol car.

Although the town was going to be in a full uproar about the drama of the sheriff's truck getting totaled, Reese hoped she could slink away back to the shop and stay out of the headlines. Reese stepped back inside her shop, where a sigh finally left her lips. What a fucking night.

Thirteen

*I sit in the shadows, my breath catching
every time she moves. I watch her, tracing
each flick of her hair, every casual glance
over her shoulder, with an intensity that
feels like it might consume me. It's like
we're connected by a thin, fragile ribbon,
one that I'm always so close to snapping.*

HE'D NEVER BEEN ONE TO FIXATE ON ANYONE
before, but since the moment he saw Reese in a Denver
newspaper, a mere flicker of interest had ignited into an
all-consuming blaze of obsession. He couldn't deny the
intensity of his feelings; they surpassed reason, eclipsing
any sense of normalcy. Reese's passion for painting had ini-
tially drawn him in, each captured moment a testament to
her artistry and grace. Unbeknownst to her, he had found
himself captivated, envisioning her as a prized possession, a
delicate masterpiece deserving of his undivided attention.
He coveted her like a polished trophy in a case—the met-

aphorical case being her shop, which was now dimly lit by the fading lights.

He stood, observing Reese as she started cleaning the shop. She'd made sure to lock the shop after the last customer.

Very smart woman, he thought. He'd been keeping an eye on Reese for the last few weeks and knew her routine. In the morning she would wake up at six, have a cup of tea in her shop, and start the day with an apple or a similar fruit. She would post up on one of the corner chairs near the shop windows and do a myriad of tasks while eating her breakfast.

He had seen the way she flushed with color every time the sheriff looked at her, and as he watched the sheriff effortlessly charm Reese with his easy smile and witty banter, a dark seed of jealousy took root in his chest. Every laugh she shared with the sheriff felt like a knife twisting deeper into his gut. The possessive urge to reclaim her attention consumed him, overshadowing reason with a burning desire to prove himself worthy in her eyes once more. His obsession with Reese was growing into a blazing inferno, enveloping everything he did.

He had stolen *Bound* the night of her store opening. He'd done his research on Reese's shop and knew she didn't have cameras. If he wiggled the back entrance door enough, the lock would come loose—something he would have told Reese about. But he decided to keep that information to himself. Selfish of him, he knew. He had hung *Bound* above his large fireplace. It was a perfect spot for it to live: in front of everything, a statement piece for sure.

There would be a day when Reese would see her art on his wall, and she would love where it was living. He felt no remorse for stealing from the woman he was protecting.

As he continued looking at the shop, Reese finished wiping down the bar top, and he knew, like clockwork, she would be in the shower in a few moments. He made his way around to the back of the building. He eyed her Barracuda, covered and tucked behind her shop. He knew she loved that car; it always looked immaculate, and its shine was a huge contrast to the dull white leather interior.

He had found that stepping farther away from the building and the parking lights gave him a view of the frosted window that opened up into the shower. Although he couldn't see anything, he always hoped Reese would show off her petite figure, just for him.

The lights flipped on in the bathroom, and a cloudy silhouette of Reese stepped closer to the window. He watched as her hands distinctly washed away the suds in her hair. He imagined being inside the shower with her. If only he could touch her, could caress her tiny waist. Just as soon as the lights flipped on, they flipped back off. Had he gotten lost in his thoughts?

"That was a fast shower, Reese," he said to himself.

He waited for the side window that led into her bedroom to light up, but something was strange. She didn't turn on the lights like normal. He hesitated for a few more moments, waiting to see where she would go inside her shop.

Is she playing hard to get? Just as he was starting to wonder if she had gone straight to bed, he heard the bells on the shop door ring. She was going outside. *That's strange.* He made sure to stay silent as he stalked toward the front of the building.

As soon as he peeked around the corner, he noticed the sheriff's vehicle.

Goddammit. How had he not seen the sheriff's truck? He couldn't be this reckless again.

He looked on as Reese stepped toward the truck and offered the sheriff a tea. He wished he were a bit closer so he could hear what she was saying. Whatever it was had made the sheriff get out of his truck.

Oh no, they were going back inside. This was even worse than he'd thought.

As they made their way inside, he moved to the opposite side of the street, where he stood in complete darkness. He was lucky this town hadn't had a huge boom of people, otherwise there would be more people out, and maybe even more lighting in the town at night.

He continued to watch in the dark as Reese and the sheriff spent a few hours together. What started as a nice gift of tea turned into laughing and kissing, and now Reese was straddling the sheriff in her shop. They were right in front of the window, putting on a show for everyone to see. It filled him with rage.

His heart thumped faster inside his chest as he imagined himself on the couch with Reese. Surely he would be the one to make the first move, though some part of him knew Reese wasn't the shy, innocent type. He started to get lost in the thought of Reese sliding into his lap, waiting for him, almost begging him to kiss her. He could imagine running his hands down her smooth thighs. His illusion of her on top of him, the feeling of her warm skin on his, fueled his eyes to keep watching.

He shook himself back to the present moment. How could the sheriff be her type? At best, he was just a bumbling hand of the law.

He began to spiral as he watched Reese play out exactly what he wanted, but with the sheriff. His anger overtook him. He had to do something. There had to be something he could do. He had to stop them from taking it further.

Without a second thought, he pulled out his camera and took a picture. Another keepsake of Reese—and better yet, a picture said a thousand words. He could use this in the future.

An instant after the flash, like fate, a major distraction pulled the two apart. When his camera flashed, Cody's drunk driving did the trick.

The smack of crumpling metal pierced his ears. The town would be out in force tonight after the two cars melded together. He smiled to himself. This was perfect!

He waited as Reese and the sheriff stepped out into the cold night. The town came alive, as this was a scene no one wanted to miss. But his thoughts began to unfurl.

Cody was screaming about a flash. He—and only he— knew what he was talking about. Cody had seen him.

Not only did he have to pay Cody a visit, but he had to get the sheriff out of the picture too.

Challenge accepted, Reese, he thought as he stepped off into the night. Reese was making it hard for him, but he was more than willing to have her as his.

As the darkness fell around him, he knew his next move.

Fourteen

REESE LAY IN BED FOR A MOMENT, REFLECTING ON last night. Something in the air was heavy. She'd enjoyed being so close with Shance, and her desire for him hadn't subsided. Even watching him work last night cleaning up drunk Cody was something she couldn't get out of her mind. *He was almost too good at manhandling Cody*, she thought.

Cody, who would not stop screaming about how it wasn't his fault. Something in Reese's mind echoed something Cody had shouted.

"A flash!" he'd screamed.

Was it the same flash Reese had seen through her closed eyelids? It couldn't have been anything more than Cody hitting Shance's truck, right? Something in her mind told her that something else was there. Even though Cody was drunk, she'd seen the flash too. Something piqued her interest. Could it have been another flash of a camera? She'd have to ask Shance if he'd seen a flash too.

There was no time like the present. She had to get out of bed even though her body wanted her to sleep in. Reese fought the urge to close the shop for the day and get ready for her trip back down to Denver for her art show. The show would be her first solo exhibit; normally the galleries she had been featured in had a plethora of other artists featured as well. The show was to be held at the Sanctuary of Arts, an old church building that had been turned into a gallery, which some found sacrilegious. Reese didn't mind it; she'd always had an affinity for old buildings, even if she didn't understand why.

The art director for the show had been in contact with Reese. Alexi was what one might imagine an art director would look like: very posh, borderline snobby, and always well-kept. Reese didn't mind working with him, although something always seemed more important to him, and Reese's questions and even her presence seemed to go unnoticed.

Reese's phone buzzed. *Speak of the devil*, she thought.

The text read, "Reese, so glad to have you back in Denver. There's been a major uproar about your art. The buyer from your last collection confirmed he'll be there, and from the sounds of it, he's planning on another major purchase. He requested new pieces from you specifically."

Reese couldn't help but think of who this buyer was. She hadn't met him; she'd only heard of her collection being bought after the show, when Alexi told her she'd sold a collection.

Reese didn't respond to Alexi. A slight panic hit her, as she wasn't sure what "new" pieces she was going to enter.

Stepping down the stairs to the gallery, she looked at the gallery walls, where there was still a space blank from *Bound*. As she inspected the pieces, her gaze fell on *Han-*

nah. Hannah's murder might be the inspiration Reese needed. Without another thought, Reese grabbed her supplies from the closet and dropped a tarp onto the gallery floor.

Reese didn't bother unlocking the shop today, nor did she write a Closed sign to post on the door. Reese stayed in the grasp of the creative headspace for several hours, not taking a break to eat or drink. Before she knew it, the sun was starting to dip behind the high peaks, and the valley seemed to pull the wet fog into the town as if Blue Sky were drowning in a lake of dense clouds.

Reese leaned back and stretched, looking to the darkened main street from her gallery. She sighed, realizing she'd spent the entire day working on a new piece. She stepped back and stared at her latest painting. It was of a woman grasping at her neck with a red ribbon around it. Reese wasn't convinced that this piece would sell or even be something that the world accepted as art. A sting of discouragement hit her chest. She had to get out of the shop, at least until she could erase her disappointment. She had decided to go for a drive to clear her head and rid herself of that familiar taste of second-guessing herself.

Reese shuffled through the shop, leaving her mess in the gallery; it was something for future Reese to deal with.

It was nearly dark outside, and the fog sure didn't help. With it being so late, Reese decided make the trek to the neighboring town, Zircon. Reese pushed herself out of her shop and locked it behind her.

She made her way to her beloved car. She uncovered the shiny Barracuda, and even in the dark night, her car reflected the streetlamps. Reese looked around before getting in. The fog seemed to surround the darkened streets. She tasted the dense fog on her tongue, and even the smell reminded her of a moist sponge dampening the air. Reese slid into her car and started the purring motor. She loved the roar of her car as it started. She'd put her blood, sweat, and tears into this car. It had started as a project with her father when she was younger, but it grew into a full-blown obsession when she was out of high school.

Reese whipped her car out of the main stretch of town and headed south to Zircon. As she pulled onto the main highway, she noted that there was barely anyone on the road.

Maybe the fog scares the locals, Reese thought. The all-consuming fog felt like something out of a horror movie.

Reese spent the next thirty minutes winding through the deep canyons, making her way to Zircon, getting lost in daydreams about the mountain fog, which seemed to creep on either side of her bright headlights.

Reese made the final turn into the valley where Zircon was nestled. She had been to Zircon a few times before, mainly for her late-night drives and to go to the larger stores.

Like many other small mountain towns in Colorado, Zircon was an old mining settlement turned tourist destination. Zircon got its name from the old zircon mine just north of the townsite. In the 1800s, the mine location was originally thought to contain the highest-quality gold, but when the miners brought down the deep red zircon, the township became known for its beautiful zircon mineral specimens.

The tourism was what kept Zircon afloat now. The

roaring river that whipped through the town's center kept the white-water-rafting enthusiasts busy, and the many restaurants and breweries kept them full and happy after their adventures. Zircon felt lively and young compared to Blue Sky.

Reese pulled into the large market parking lot just as the last car was pulling out. She hated going into businesses right before they closed, but luckily, the late hours of the Zircon market allowed her to have an hour before the store's lights would go off. Nevertheless, Reese didn't want to put anyone out, so she quickly grabbed a new hairbrush and a few small items to make a fast dinner with.

Before Reese knew it, she was walking back outside. Just as she reached her car, the parking lot lights shut off in a surge of power. Reese jumped, startled by the sudden darkness that surrounded her.

As she relaxed her now-thumping heart, bright lights from across the large parking lot flashed on her, as if Reese were onstage. She shielded her eyes from the lights, which made her eyes throb. She tried squinting to see past the bright lights and noticed three sets of lights coming from what she believed to be a large truck.

The lights sitting on top of the roof of the vehicle were so bright that her eyes started to water just staring at them. There were also the regular headlights and a set of smaller ditch lights. If this truck were to pull behind her, she'd be blinded and run off the road.

As Reese held her free hand in front of her eyes, trying to block the jarring bright lights, a roar from the diesel cut through the night. The fog seemed to pull closer to the ground, making a thick curtain below the bumper of the truck. The truck roared again, and this time Reese felt it in her chest. Whoever was inside the vehicle was revving it up to a point where the large truck sounded like it was going to lurch toward her. The tires squealed as the truck began to peel out in a cloud of burnt rubber.

Reese's heart thudded, causing her to become acutely aware of her heartbeat. It felt like the rumbling of the truck was in her chest, strangling her heart. Something wasn't right.

As Reese reached down and fumbled for her keys, the bright lights seemed to warm her, almost burning her skin. Reese couldn't control her fingers; she was becoming nervous, nearly shaking. At that moment, she heard the squealing tires lurch forward. The full power of the diesel engine now hit her ears.

Reese couldn't control her body any longer. She dropped her groceries onto the ground and fumbled through her pockets with desperate hands. The revving became louder. This person was either trying to play a prank on her or was trying to run her over. Either way, in Reese's head, the safest and only close place was inside her car. She started to pant in fear.

Cold metal hit her middle finger, and she plunged her hand deeper into her pocket, finally wrapping her fingers around the keys. Reese pulled the keys from her pocket and swung them in front of her. As she did, her fingers fumbled the keys. The ear-piercing noise of the metal keys hitting the ground struck her ears. Reese plummeted to the ground and reached for the keys she'd foolishly dropped. Lying flat, she stretched forward and looped her keys in her hand. A wave of adrenaline hit her chest.

Reese rolled to her knees and quickly unlocked her car, the truck now closer. Jumping inside without a second thought, Reese threw herself down into the bench seat and held her head in her hands, knowing she was about to become sliced deli meat. For a second, she kept her eyes open. The lights got brighter and brighter as the truck thundered closer.

Reese held her breath and forced her eyes shut, rolling farther into the seat as best she could. She took one last breath, inhaling the sweet fumes of the heavy diesel.

If death smelled like diesel fumes and burning tires, so be it.

Fifteen

REESE CLENCHED HER EYES AS TIGHT AS SHE COULD. Her heart thudded hard in her chest. The smell of diesel was thick in the air, but something odd hit her ears. The diesel engine seemed to come to a lull. Her eyes burned as she slowly lifted her eyelids and removed her hands from her face.

She was still alive.

Her body was in shock, and she didn't know if what had just happened was real. The faint smell of burning rubber still hung in the air.

Reese shook herself. She was alive, and the most important thing to do now was to get out of there. Just as Reese's mind came back to earth, a tap on the window stung her ears. Reese whirled to look to the driver's side, where a bright light blinded her, causing her to shield her eyes once more.

Reese studied the light through her splayed fingers and made out a figure standing in front of her.

Shance.

Shance stood there in his dark uniform, his cowboy hat casting shadows off his shoulders and over her. Reese reached for the window crank and rolled the window down. Shance stood eagerly waiting with his new patrol truck's bright lights pinned on Reese's car.

Something uneasy squeezed Reese's chest. Had Shance just tried to run her over? The lights on his patrol truck had a striking resemblance to the truck from before.

Shance took a step back. "Reese, what are you doing here?"

"I was just getting some last-minute things for my trip to Denver. What are you doing here?" Her words were blatantly accusatory.

"I'm on duty; you're still in my county." Shance became defensive, reflecting her tone.

If he'd tried to run her over, it would be best if she didn't poke the bear.

Reese shook her head. "Sorry, Shance. I just . . ." She stopped and stared into his blue eyes. "I just dropped my keys into the wheel well."

Shance lowered his flashlight, staring at her. "Are you okay?"

Reese nodded, not saying a word.

"Okay. I just saw a huge plume of smoke and heard tires squealing. Are you sure you're okay?"

"Sorry, I was just playing around. Blue Sky doesn't have any open parking lots like this one." Reese pulled out another bullshit excuse. The more she waited in her car, the more her mind started to convince her that something wasn't right with Shance. How had he gotten there so fast? How had he not seen another truck trying to run her over?

And how had she not noticed the light bars on the patrol trucks before?

Reese was paralyzed with fear, her heart still pumping in her throat, nearly choking her. She could barely swallow as she stared at Shance.

He nodded. "Well, next time please don't leave tire tracks so deep. I already know the store owner is going to call us tomorrow to complain." He nodded to the deep black marks left on the blacktop.

Reese swallowed.

"Are you sure you're okay?" Shance asked once again, turning back to her.

"I'm okay. I'd better get back," she stated dryly.

SHANCE STEPPED BACK, NOT SAYING ANOTHER WORD as Reese started her thundering car. He watched as she drove off into the night, then stepped toward the tire tracks across the parking lot from where Reese's car had been parked. Shance knelt down, his fingers sticking to the warm tire tread that led straight to where Reese's groceries lay. The bag was slumped to one side, her groceries nearly escaping from the bag. The scene made Shance shudder.

He stood, rubbing the tire tread off his fingers. The tire tracks were too large to have come from Reese's car. Why hadn't she told him the truth of what had happened moments before he was there? He couldn't think of why she would hide something like this from him; he just wished he'd been there sooner to see what had happened. The smell of the burnt tires singed his nose, along with an undertone of diesel. He reflected on the smoke he'd seen billowing out from the parking lot before he'd responded. At first he'd thought the grocery store was on fire.

He followed the tire tracks to where Reese's groceries lay. Shance picked up the groceries before turning back to the tire tracks. He knew Reese was in danger; something inside his chest told him so. It wasn't anything concrete or even something he could verbalize, but in his heart he knew something was off. This was what made him a good sheriff: his gut never steered him wrong.

Shance swung open his driver's side door and flung Reese's groceries into the passenger's seat. He turned once more to the tire tracks, and without another thought, he took out his camera and snapped a few pictures of the tread pattern scarred across the parking lot.

Shance was determined to keep Reese around. He'd only had a brief taste of her last night, but that taste was something he couldn't get out of his mind. She smelled like lilac and pomegranate and tasted even sweeter. He knew this incident was related to everything going on with her shop, and if Reese wasn't going to save herself, he would.

Sixteen

THE NEXT MORNING, SHANCE COULDN'T SLEEP, HE was anxious to see Reese, even after working his late shift. He had held on to her groceries for her; if anything, that was a good excuse to at least see her. He knew she was going to leave for Denver tomorrow for her art show, which he had done his research on. It was on Broadway, one of Denver's main arteries. He was looking into hotels near the art show, but to his disgust, the only hotels available were more expensive than an airplane ticket to the Bahamas. He'd been pondering the thought of going to see Reese at the show, even if she had dodged him last night, putting up her icy walls. He had convinced himself that even if she didn't want him there, he was still going to be close. He was becoming more and more enthralled with Reese; just the refreshing energy of being around her made him want to linger just a bit more every time he saw her. Was he becoming clouded with passion?

Last night echoed in his head. Shance kept thinking of the tire tracks. Something wasn't right, and in his gut he knew someone was either targeting her or trying to scare her. Either way, Shance felt defensive; he didn't want anyone to hurt or terrorize Reese. His heart sank. He hadn't felt anything like this before for anyone. Shance sat on his bed, reflecting on the beautiful woman who plagued his mind and body.

Shance stood from the bed and slid into the pair of dark blue jeans that had been flung over a large chair near the bed. Shance pulled the waistband past his tight Adonis belt muscle. He'd always loved how well his hips and flat stomach came together in a V shape above his pelvis. He hadn't even paid any attention to the name of the muscle until recently when he started to perfect his body. He grabbed a flannel shirt, hiding his toned chest beneath the warm fabric. Shance pulled on his dark boots, tucking them into his pants, then stepped into the kitchen, looking at the small bag of groceries sitting on his counter.

Everything he looked at reminded him of Reese. Even simple delicate smells reminded him of her.

REESE HAD BARELY SLEPT. THE WIND SCRATCHING on her windows had kept her eyes from closing, and even the subtle noises of her shop settling had jolted her awake. Reese was on edge. She was even considering getting a dog or cat, a companion to keep her and her shop safe. She remembered Hannah had had a dog, and that hadn't stopped the killer from getting her. She started to feel disheartened and utterly alone.

She wasn't sure how to feel about Shance. Had he tried to run her over? She couldn't see how it was possible that

Shance had gotten there so fast, especially if he hadn't seen anything—or acted like it anyway. Maybe Shance knew something she didn't know. Maybe he had seen someone driving toward her in the thick smoke and fog. If that was the case, Shance knew she had lied to him about doing burnouts in her car.

Reese felt a bit guilty, and she was afraid she may have ruined her chances with Shance. The thought weighed her down, making her head feel heavy.

Reese was clouded in confusion; she didn't know what to think. And like many times before, she knew that the only way out of the insufferable daze that held her mind and body in its grasp was to put up the cold defense.

Maybe all of this will blow over, she thought. If anything, her way of coping might actually be the best idea for her mentally. She couldn't stand the way last night had made her feel; it was as if her world had been flipped on her.

Reese slipped out of bed and began getting ready for the day. She put on some tight blue jeans and a black hoodie with a design of her art on the front. Looking in the mirror, she found that her chocolate hair seemed flat—or maybe she was projecting that onto her reflection. Either way, she didn't want to deal with the mess that was her hair. Reese pulled her hair up into a swift messy bun that sat on top of her head, then made her way down to her shop floor.

Reese peeked outside to find that the main street was nearly abandoned. The cold frost of the morning clung to the small buildings, roads, and even to the lavender plants she had planted. Winter was coming.

It was early, but she still had some preparation to do for tomorrow. Reese started getting her things together and organizing them for the Denver show. She had to concentrate on things to come, not the strange few nights she'd just had.

Reese spent a few hours cleaning up the shop, including her gallery. She then got her small luggage packed, though she still felt as if she had forgotten something. Her hairbrush and her groceries.

Damn it. If Shance had seen her leave her groceries, her story wouldn't add up for sure.

Reese couldn't think about that now. She had to distract herself in some way, and the only way she saw was to open her shop like normal.

Act normal, she thought. Reese didn't have anything to hide, but Shance did.

The day went by smoothly. She served a few townies, including two women who now sat at the small table near the large bay window in the warm sun.

Just as she thought she was calm and relaxed, a shudder rolled down her back. The shop bells rang, and Shance was standing there, looking afraid to step fully inside. He must have known something was off with Reese; it didn't take a rocket scientist to figure that one out.

Reese could feel the elderly ladies' eyes burning a hole into her back. They had been coming to Reese's shop just to spill the tea on things that were happening around town. There they sat, in Reese's shop, enjoying their own figurative and metaphorical tea. Reese was fond of the two women; she loved listening in on all the town gossip, and she'd occasionally hear more juicy stories to tell to Gina, who would return the favor with some of the other happenings of Blue Sky.

Shance lowered his eyes as he stepped inside.

"Evening, Miss Reese. I just wanted to stop by and drop this off." He motioned to the grocery bag he held.

Reese reached for the bag. In a strange way, the bag of groceries was the one thing holding them together.

"Thank you. I was wondering what I'd done with this," Reese said, blowing off the apparent tension between them.

Good job, girl. Deep breath, she coached herself.

Reese placed the groceries onto the counter, aware of the deafening silence from the two women, who were obviously listening to every word and picking up on the uneasiness between her and Shance.

"Reese, we need to talk," he said as he stepped farther into the shop, motioning for her to move away from the two ladies, probably knowing full well they were listening too.

"Are you two ladies going to be okay for a bit?" Reese asked the women. They blushed, and one made a shooing motion as she smiled up at Reese.

Reese and Shance made their way to the back where the gallery was.

"Did you get robbed again?" Shance asked, gaze trained on the bare walls.

"Oh, no, of course not. I'm getting ready for the trip down to Denver tomorrow," Reese explained as she dropped the small curtains that separated the gallery from the shop.

Shance turned back to her. "Well, we need to talk about last night."

Reese leaned against the doorframe, her arms crossed, instinctually protecting herself from him. Although Reese felt very vulnerable, she was more so confused. "Okay?" she questioned him in a low tone, trying to keep her skin from crawling away from her.

"I know you didn't do a burnout in that parking lot last night," Shance stated matter-of-factly, his eyes beaming toward her in confidence.

Damn, Reese thought. How could she spin this, or should she spin this at all? If Shance had tried to run her over, why would he be here interrogating her?

"You're right," she confirmed. "I panicked, thinking you'd tried to run me over. I wanted to get out of there as fast as I could."

A weight lifted from the surrounding air. Honesty was the best answer.

Shance's eyes widened, and he cocked his head in confusion. "Wait, back up. What makes you believe someone was going to run you over?"

Reese drew in a deep breath. "I was walking back to my car when this truck started up and blinded me with its lights. It started revving up and took off toward me. If you hadn't been there, I think I'd be forever engraved on the seats of my car."

"Reese, I don't think you should go to Denver," Shance said, sounding angry. "There are too many strange things happening to you, including the fact you were almost killed. I want to stay close by to make sure you don't end up as roadkill."

His words were harsh, and they stung Reese's ears.

She didn't want to hear that the art show was no longer on the table.

"Also, you can't keep hiding these things from me. We

need to find out who's terrorizing you," he said, coming closer to her.

Reese was still reeling from hearing Shance say she shouldn't go to Denver. Having a heavy make-out session didn't mean she was his. Fury rose inside her.

"I'm going to Denver; I have too much on the line to say no to this show, and you know that." Reese hoped her words stung him just as much as his words had poked at her. She couldn't believe he'd even suggested that she not go to her own art show. The fact that Shance had ignored their lengthy conversation about how much her art had changed her life and how much the show meant to her was proof that this man was oblivious or only thought of himself.

At the same time, doubt welled in her chest as she reconsidered what he had just said. What if someone was after her? What if she was in danger? Reese's thoughts danced around as she wondered what she could do to protect herself.

"Goddammit, Reese. Can't you see that I'm trying to keep you safe?" Shance's eyes narrowed, pulling Reese back into the present conversation.

That statement stung. Reese stood with her arms still crossed as if she were protecting her heart, herself. Reese drew in a deep breath, but before she could say anything else, Shance interjected.

"If you're not going to listen to my warnings, that's on you. But I'll be fucking damned if I let anything happen to you." Shance walked past her, bumping her shoulder, nearly knocking her off-balance. Reese spun to see him push the gallery curtains aside in a childish fit. Shance nodded to the blue-haired women. "Ladies," he murmured before storming out of the shop.

The two ladies started whispering. That was just what Reese needed: more drama surrounding her shop. Anger welled up inside her. She doubted it'd been Shance's intention to cause more drama for Reese—that wasn't his style—but at the same time, she wouldn't put it past him either if he was feeling squirrely.

Reese tucked the curtains to the side once again, opening up the gallery to more light, then stepped into the shop to face the two women. Reese did what she did best and tried to kill their gossip with her hospitality. She refilled their drinks on the house and brought them some fresh fruit.

As much as Reese tried to curb their gossip, she knew as soon as the women left they would be telling their book club, or worse: the knitting club Gina had warned Reese about.

Reese had a hard time concentrating on anything more than the strange interaction with Shance. She was thinking of any action she could take to smooth things over with him, but she stood by her decision to go to Denver.

Reese couldn't risk missing out on a possible payday if the art buyer was just as interested in her new series as her last. It wasn't about the money though; as much as she wanted the money and hoped the buyer would invest more in her, she enjoyed creating pieces.

She saw her art as an escape, and the places her paintings could take her were nothing of this reality. It was like a form of deep meditation. Even if the art buyer didn't purchase a single piece of hers, she was still looking forward to getting out of Blue Sky. She wanted an escape. Although she loved Blue Sky, Denver was looking like a welcome vacation from the slow times. Denver was the city of pioneers—well, the pioneers who'd looked to the foothills and said, "Nope." Something about that statement made Reese smile as she imagined pioneers seeing the rugged mountains and being so secure in themselves to just admit defeat and settle in the flatlands.

So she settled as well.

She was going to Denver.

Seventeen

IF THE SHEER SIGHT OF HOUSING BUMPING AGAINST the highway was any indication, Denver had grown even in just the few months Reese had been gone. As soon as her eyes hit the flat brown part of the plains from the high peak of the highway, she knew she was going to regret going to Denver. She felt that same sense of community and that fleeting feeling of being safe as her gaze settled on the large city in front of her. Shance was right.

The streets were packed with more people and cars than Reese remembered. It was a slight culture shock coming back down to the city after living in small-town America for the past few months. The day seemed unseasonably warm, although most of the days in Denver now felt like a mild eighty degrees, especially in the city.

When cars zoomed by, familiar heat radiated off the black-tar pavement. The sheer number of people even seemed to warm the city from the ground up. Reese had forgotten how the heat seemed to rise from the pavement in waves, enveloping the sprawling downtown in a heavy,

suffocating warmth. The city streets, crowded with concrete and steel, radiated the day's heat, making the air feel
thick and alive with a pulsating energy.

She pulled over next to the gallery on Broadway where
her show was going to be, her Barracuda still purring
warmly. Her gaze rolled up and down the large Gothic pil-
lars casting shade on Broadway.

Gina pulled behind her in her SUV. Gina had followed Reese to Denver, not only to help transport her
paintings, but Reese suspected Gina had come to Denver
just to see Alexi.

The two women exited their vehicles. Gina immediately
opened her trunk, where the paintings were. Gina stepped
inside the gallery, Reese assumed to find where to unload
her paintings.

Reese stepped to the back of Gina's SUV. Where she
started unloading her paintings, when a cold shadow rose
from her feet to block the dry autumn sun.

Reese turned to see Alexi's shadow nearly peeling away
from him as he continued toward her in a feline strut that
screamed, "I'm a confident gay man, hear me roar."

Alexi's mouth quirked. He rarely smiled, and when he
did, it usually meant something was going wrong or he was
conspiring with someone.

"Afternoon, Reese." His voice was thick with the East-
ern European accent that Reese had a hard time decipher-
ing, especially when Alexi had any form of booze in his sys-
tem. He was bound to drink at these art shows—maybe a
bit too much for Reese's liking.

Reese greeted Alexi with a delicate hug from the side.

"Here, let me help you unload these." Alexi's hands moved from Reese to grab the paintings that filled Gina's entire SUV from the front seats to the trunk.

Gina had then walked back outside from the gallery. Her face lit up when she saw Alexi.

"Alexi!" Gina soon was in a full-on sprint, nearly galloping to Alexi. Although Reese had never been super close with Alexi, Gina had made it her mission to always find him at parties in Denver because, well, he was Gina's type of person: chic, posh, and a hard-core partier, the type of person who seemed to make Gina's life in Blue Sky feel like *Little House on the Prairie*.

Alexi and Gina embraced each other, then kissed each other's cheeks, one on each side. Both Alexi and Gina started whining about how much work the show was going to be and how if it were up to them, they wouldn't lift a finger and just drink the entire night, judging those around them based on what type of clothes or shoes they were wearing.

At that moment, Reese wished she had never introduced the two. Her cynical nature was showing through. Reese handed each of them a canvas, and before she could hand them another to carry inside, Alexi and Gina, so wrapped up in their superficial conversation, headed back inside the church. The gabbing about the latest trends and the hottest gossip faded to a dull murmur. Reese was left standing there, staring at the pile of art she now was unloading alone.

As Reese's thoughts became clouded with a tinge of anger, and maybe a bit of jealousy, a larger shadow hit her feet. She turned to face the source of the darked sun, thinking Gina had realized she had ditched her friend to load the remaining pieces.

To Reese's surprise, a harmonious voice surrounded her.

"Looks like you could use some help." The first thing Reese noticed was the man's nearly black hair, which fell past his shoulders and down his back, tied neatly together at the base of his neck. The tight black curls made Reese's mind play with the idea of what his hair would look like falling freely around his face—wild and primal, she wagered.

The man's eyes were shrouded in dark sunglasses that cast shadows down his shapely jawline. Intrigued, Reese wondered what color was behind those dark glasses. A small dark beard scruffed his face, causing him to look a bit more rugged than clean-cut. He wore a pressed and fitted white dress shirt that flattered his toned shoulders and dark blue dress slacks that looked like they were tailored just for him. He looked fancy.

Reese shook herself out of her thoughts. "I wouldn't mind the help, but I don't want you to get your nice shirt dirty." Shrugging, she went back to grabbing a few more pieces.

"Please, I insist," the man retorted, reaching for the pieces Reese had set on the ground next to Gina's car. As the man came closer, a wall of incredibly masculine scent hit Reese's nose.

The smell danced under her nose, a tempting fragrance of cedarwood and espresso. It smelled as if it was curated just for him. Reese didn't doubt that everything he wore had been made specifically for him and him alone; he screamed money. At the same time, even though he wore the right outfit to flatter his muscular arms and the right shirt that made his tanned complexion seem as smooth as if he had baby-soft skin, Reese had to pull herself back before her mind wandered too deep, slipping into the labyrinth of her thoughts.

Reese shook herself again. "Oh, thank you. I'm Reese." She tried to be polite and mask her true thoughts of the man standing next to her.

The man held out his hand. "Devin."

His name rolled off his tongue with pride. Reese could tell his confidence leaked through everything he touched and did. Reese placed her hand in his, his touch so warm and welcoming. A small smirk cracked at the side of his mouth, a sly smile that could melt a woman's heart. Reese had to pull her hand from his almost instantly, as she felt her body start to spark with warmth from touching his smooth hand.

"Thank you again. You look awfully familiar." It felt like she had seen him before, or maybe his straight jawline resembled a male model she vaguely remembered.

"I don't think we've ever met, but I do know your work." He turned back to the pieces that lay in front of him. "This one is new," he said, motioning to the painting of Hannah, which was covered in the see-through wrap that protected the paintings from getting banged up in the car.

"I finished this one in memory of Hannah Franklin, who was murdered in Blue Sky," Reese said as she looked to the man to see his reaction.

"I did hear about her. She was all over the news. They still haven't caught her killer, right?" Devin quirked his head toward Reese.

"That's right. Blue Sky is still on edge." Still thinking of how someone could have taken Hannah's life, Reese grabbed the painting and tucked it under her arm. She made a motion to shut the SUV trunk, and Devin grabbed a few paintings and followed her toward the Sanctuary of Arts.

Reese stepped inside the cold, damp-feeling building. Her eyes meandered throughout the darkened room, taking in every detail of the old church's nave. The cream-colored archways on each side and three larger archways in the center of the room made Reese feel so small in a flash. The room was lit with a multitude of colorful stage lights that were normally used for the nightlife scene. The intricate hand-carved details on the dark beams running across the ceiling were mind-boggling.

Reese stood for a moment just staring at the room her art was going to have the opportunity to hang inside. This place was amazing. She was still astonished that she was able to make such a huge show. She had the art buyer to thank for that. Reese didn't even know his name.

No matter how much Reese had begged Alexi, he'd never told her the buyer's name. Reese had borderline harassed Alexi for months about the art buyer, and the only information that he had divulged was that the art buyer was a wealthy man. Unfortunately, that didn't narrow it down for Reese. Something inside her was looking forward to tomorrow night; maybe she'd finally meet the guy.

Alexi walked toward Reese, his eyes narrowed. "I see you've met Devin." The statement made Reese question his tone. Something was off.

"Yeah, he was nice enough to help me inside with everything." The little jab at Alexi made Reese feel warm and fuzzy on the inside; she was still mad that he and Gina had just left her on the street unloading by herself.

Before Reese could fire any more verbal shots at Alexi, Devin set the paintings to the side and took the hint to see himself out. He said his goodbyes to Reese and Alexi, then made his way back to the entrance, where he passed Gina, whose jaw dropped involuntarily as he brushed by her. Reese knew that face: Gina was about to say something crude and sexual. Sure enough, Gina smirked and, without missing a beat, said, "If that man got any closer, I'd have to charge him rent for living in my fantasies!" She hinted at more comments she would make about Devin's body and the things she would do to him if given the chance, with that same smirk and a sly wink. Reese performed an entire body-size eye roll at Gina.

The next few hours were spent with Alexi, who explained how the show was to go. Although Reese didn't really need to know every exact detail, she liked knowing what was planned and who was expected to be there.

To Reese's surprise, there was more media attention about this show than she'd expected, not only for the fact that she may be selling more art to this mysterious art buyer who was expected to be at the show, but also because *Hannah* had gained national attention due to the ongoing investigation into Hannah's death. Even the fact the sheriff's department didn't have any leads, also sent the local reporters into a frenzy.

From Reese's understanding, Shance had been working the case, but he'd also been seeing her almost every day for the past few months. Shance's warning echoed in her head—his words encouraging Reese not to go through with this art show for fear it might be dangerous, not only for her, but for everyone who attended the event. There was a real possibility that the killer could attend tomorrow night. The thought sent shivers down Reese's spine.

Reese had made the decision to continue with the art show, showing off *Hannah*, keeping her eyes on the audience once again. She wasn't a detective, but she knew the best way to bait a killer was to get their attention, one way or another. She'd started sounding like Shance: *trying to bait a killer.*

Eighteen

THE FOLLOWING EVENING, REESE'S NERVES WERE at an all-time high. She was damn near shaking and could barely concentrate on curling her hair and getting dressed without having the pit in her stomach eat away at her.

What if something happened tonight? How would she be able to handle whatever it was?

In the back of her mind, she knew that if something was going to happen, it probably wasn't going to happen in front of everyone . . . hopefully. Part of her doubted her confidence, not only as the singular artist featured in the show but also as a woman. Her gut told her the darkness was setting in. As Reese poked small black-pearl earrings into her ears, there was a knock at her hotel door, disrupting her thoughts.

Reese stalked toward the hotel door and peeked through the peephole. Her heart dropped when she saw Shance standing in the hallway. For a moment, she hesitated, thinking of the reasons not to let him in. He'd nearly demanded that Reese not leave Blue Sky. Something was still off about that entire conversation, and they hadn't left it on a good note. Reese took a deep breath as she unlocked the dead bolt and the chain.

"Can I help you?' Reese said with a tinge of annoyance in her voice.

"Look—" His voice cracked, and he cleared his throat. "I owe you an apology, but I have reason to believe you're in danger. Even if you don't want to see me tonight, just know I'll be at your show." Shance looked to his feet as if he was trying to conceal the color that hit his face. "I didn't want to blindside you at the show." He took a deep breath and looked up.

"If you think it'll benefit your investigation, then so be it. I can't change that. But I want you to know that I can handle my own shit." Reese moved to step back inside the room.

"I'm sorry, Reese, but you have to see where I'm coming from. There've been too many things surrounding you and your art, and it has me on edge, not to mention Hannah's killer could very well be there tonight. I can't have another dead body on my hands."

The words stung.

Reese started to feel a bit of responsibility for Hannah's death. Though she couldn't put the pieces together just yet, something had finally clicked. It was no longer wondering if the killer was targeting her. Reese began to think of everything that had happened in the last few months: Hannah's death, the theft of her art, strange flashes, and then someone trying to run her over.

Shance was right, goddammit. He was right.

Reese didn't know how she could have been so blind the last few months. She started mentally kicking herself.

"I'm sorry, Shance. I've been dodgy this entire time, but just know you're more than welcome tonight. If you see something, though, will you keep me in the loop? I don't want my show to go to shit because we're trying to catch a killer."

Shance nodded, then tipped his hat like when Reese first met him, an agreement or a promise of sorts.

The night began like most art shows, with people dressed to the nines meandering through The Sanctuary of Arts, feasting their eyes on Reese's pieces. The namesake made Reese chuckle inside. She knew how cliché all of this sounded.

Reese made it a point to take in as much as she could, including the deep red lighting, which seemed to add a certain aura to each of her paintings. The paintings were suspended from the ceiling on the outer edges of the nave on each side. Between each painting were clusters of white candles. They seemed to add a sense of life to each painting, their flickering almost causing the eyes to think the paintings were moving in a dance of flames.

Hannah hung high above the rest at the head of the church, the strange warm lights surrounding Hannah's face. The painting looked as if it had been brought to life, much like the *Mona Lisa*, but this of a woman who'd been brutally murdered.

The deep ambient music matched the atmosphere near perfectly, and the warm candlelight seemed to reflect off the tall glasses the waitstaff walked around with.

A few staff members offered deep red wine, and others offered a crisp sparkling white. The staff wore all black, as per Reese's request; those who were here for the people-watching should be invisible to the people they served—much like Reese, who also wore all black.

She wanted to blend in with the crowd, not stand above the rest. She couldn't lie to herself though—she looked damn good in her silky dress.

Her thoughts danced when she thought of the look on Shance's face when he saw her little black dress, the silk hugging her hips. She knew where his mind went when he saw her. Reese knew he would be here tonight and wondered if he would still be wearing a cowboy hat or if he was smart enough to know he would stand out like a sore thumb in Denver with it on.

Before Reese knew it, Alexi grabbed her arm and pulled her through the curtains of the staging room of the gallery. The deep velvet curtains from the outside seemed so solid, but when Reese entered, she noticed a somewhat sheer sensation as she watched the gallery. She could see the small crowd grow as their shadows danced on the curtains she now hid behind. She felt nearly invisible. Alexi tried to explain what was going on, but Reese didn't hear a word. She was too focused on people-watching through the curtains that hid her and Alexi.

Alexi grabbed her shoulders and shook her. "Reese! Pay attention!" His voice broke her dreamy state. "Your Hannah piece, the one you said was not going to be for sale *ever*, just received an offer. A very large offer." He took a deep breath. The offer of a lifetime for him. "A million dollars."

Reese blinked, hardly knowing what to say. Sure, she had sold an entire collection before, but there was no way this was real. She still didn't believe her art was even good enough to be hanging in this gallery, and yet here she was, getting offers on art that even now dumbfounded her.

"I have to take a second, Alexi. This is too much." Reese swallowed, pushing Alexi away and moving though the darkened room.

Reese didn't know how to think, but something in her head told her to go tell Shance. Where was he? She hadn't seen him yet. Reese stepped lightly around the nave, grabbing a glass of red wine from one of the waitstaff. She slammed the wine in one gulp and set the glass back on the tray.

Reese looked all around, but she didn't pinpoint any familiar faces. Until she looked toward the rear of the nave, where Shance stood leaning against the stone wall.

As she started toward him, she took in his every detail. Though his rough cowboy exterior was what she was used to, even now, the deep grape-merlot shirt cut him so nice on the shoulders and chest. Something about him always seemed to scream, "I work with my hands." In his case, "working with his hands" meant tackling the baddies and getting search warrants. Reese's eyes seemed to fixate on him as he took a sip from the small glass he held, which she guessed was a good bourbon.

His ice-blue eyes seemed to scan the room, taking in every person. Reese knew he had already seen her; she'd felt his gaze on her, her body heating eagerly for him to glance at her again. Reese had to admit, he looked damn good tonight, and she was so used to seeing him in uniform. In fact, she hadn't seen him without the cowboy hat or the badge. But he looked so nice in the deep red shirt and fitted dark jeans. Reese made note that he still wore tactical boots.

"Evening, miss." Shance tilted his head as if to tip his nonexistent hat to her.

Reese curled a smile at him and turned to face away from the crowd, whose eyes always seemed to follow her no matter where she was in the room. "I have interesting information for you." Reese leaned closer to him. "I received an offer on *Hannah*. An offer that would be very suspicious to me if I were a betting man." Reese motioned back to the room facing the painting. "*Hannah* isn't for sale, and I would never sell it—it would be a disgrace to her family—but it leads me to believe that the killer might be here. Something just seems strange about the offer."

Shance turned with her, standing next to her, leaning his back against the wall once more. "What about the offer seems suspicious?" he questioned before sipping his bourbon.

"The offer was a million," Reese whispered. "That's unheard of. I realize I'm catching the attention of art critics and such, but that's a huge offer. Something tells me it's a bad deal. And I have to trust my gut."

"If you think it's a bad deal, and there's a possibility that this person is the killer, then we should explore it."

Her cheeks warmed. "I'm not setting a trap, and the painting isn't for sale. I'm just relaying to you what happened." Before Reese could continue shooting Shance's insane idea down, her nose alerted her to the presence of

Devin, the man from yesterday. The deep undertone of cedarwood seemed to be his signature, and her brain made the connection instantly.

"Excuse me, sir, may I cut in?" Devin's voice was low and even.

Shance immediately stood up straight, casting a small shadow on Devin. Shance was just a smidge taller than Devin, but the image of Shance slightly puffing his chest in front of Devin made Reese think of delicate male peacocks showing their feathers to impress the female. Reese could have sworn she heard a deep throaty growl come from Shance's throat, or maybe that was just her imagination.

That growl may have been something of truth. Shance knew something; Devin was familiar. Realization rushed across Shance's face. He knew Devin from Blue Sky, he had been at the bar the night Gina was drugged. That growl was intentional and deliberate. Shance took one gulp from his glass, then stepped away, still not completely leaving the two alone. He set his glass on a nearby standing table, and it was promptly picked up by an event server. Shance did not let Devin out of his sight; Devin was his only lead now. Devin was the only Blue Sky resident—besides himself, Gina, and Reese—that he had spotted.

With one look toward Reese, Devin smirked. His eyes were so dark that they seemed like tiny pits of black coal. Without another word, Devin began to lead Reese through the meandering crowd. Reese had noted how warm and smooth his hands were, like a brief touch from a flame. His touch was alluring. He led her directly to the center of the painting of Hannah and looked up.

"Can I be brutally honest?" Devin asked.

Reese nodded in silence, anxiously waiting for what Devin was about to say.

"I think *Hannah* is the focus of most people here, just for their sake to say they were here and they saw the picture of a murdered woman. But these other pieces directly reflect you and your talent." Devin took a step toward Reese and sighed. "You can do way better than this *Hannah* shit."

His words echoed in Reese's head for a moment, and her face went warm. Who was this man to talk? What business did he have to insult her art? He had said he'd been following her art, so maybe she might want to value his opinion.

To hell with that, she thought as she turned toward Devin.

"With all due respect, art is meant to be controversial, and the fact that *Hannah* made you feel you had to confront me about your opinion means I'm doing a great a job." Her prideful words leaked from her mouth.

Devin nodded and shot her a quick smile. For a moment, Devin was lost in his thoughts. But soon Devin's smile widened slightly as he replied, "Fair enough. If your goal was to provoke a reaction, you've succeeded. Just don't lose sight of the artist behind the controversy. You've got real talent, Reese—don't let it get buried under shock value." Devin's words sent Reese into a frenzy; she found herself questioning herself and everything she had done in the last few years. Had she not made it as an artist? She didn't want to merely discarded as a "Shock Value" artist.

Devin's smile lingered a bit too long, his eyes never quite leaving Reese. "I suppose you're right though. Art should provoke thought and stir emotions. Maybe I just got caught up in the shock of it all. But I genuinely admire your talent. It's rare to find someone with such a compelling vision. I'd love to see how far you can push those boundaries."

The thought gnawed at her. Devin's words lingered in Reese's mind as the evening continued to unfold. What followed was a whirlwind of emotions and events. She was bombarded with a massive offer for the Hannah piece, a moment that left her reeling. Meanwhile, Shance, ever the brooding sheriff, stationed himself in a corner, his watchful gaze sweeping over the crowd. Despite the chaos around her, Reese found a strange comfort in knowing Shance was there, his presence making her feel just a little bit safer.

Reese had also continued a lengthy conversation with Devin, whom she now knew was Devin Brooks, an investment banker who had funded her Blue Sky endeavors by purchasing her previous collection. Devin hadn't mentioned that, though, and he seemed to be a private, well-guarded man. Alexi had seemed to have seen Reese and Devin from afar. Although Alexi's intention was to soothe Reese, He came across as a bumbling idiot.

"Oh, Reese, my darling. I see you've met Devin—or should I say Lord Devin." His words slurred beneath him.

Reese looked to Alexi, who was now holding his billionth glass of champagne. Reese decided to play into his drunken alter ego, which she knew all too well from Gina's stories. "Alexi! So nice of you to join us. We were just speaking on how overrated *Hannah* is. What are your thoughts?" Reese smiled, knowing she had trapped him.

"If you want my honest opinion . . ." Alexi paused dramatically, swaying slightly as he struggled to focus. "*Hannah* is like . . . the *Mona Lisa* of the macabre. Overrated, overanalyzed, and yet somehow, everyone just can't stop staring at her." Reese stifled a laugh, watching as Alexi raised his glass in a sloppy toast. "But you, my darling Reese," he continued, nearly spilling his drink, "you're like . . . like the rebellious artist who painted her mustache. You bring the shock, the awe . . . the art world needs more of that!" Devin raised an eyebrow at Alexi's rambling, but there was a hint of amusement in his eyes. Reese smiled, knowing she had successfully steered the conversation away from the tension Devin had stirred.

"Well, Alexi," Reese replied with a smirk, "it's good to know you appreciate a little rebellion in art. Maybe there's hope for you yet."

Alexi chuckled, clearly pleased with himself, but his drunken state was starting to loosen his tongue more than Reese had anticipated.

"You know, Devin here isn't just some ordinary admirer," he slurred, leaning in a bit too close to Reese. "Oh, no, my dear, he's the one who dropped a fortune on your Blue Sky collection! Our very own secret millionaire—though not so secret now, eh?"

Reese's eyes widened slightly, and she glanced at Devin, who gave a slight, almost imperceptible shake of his head, as if to downplay Alexi's revelation. But the damage was done.

"Is that so?" Reese asked, her voice measured, trying to process this new information while keeping her composure.

Devin sighed, clearly not thrilled with Alexi's loose lips. "It wasn't something I planned to bring up tonight," he admitted, his voice calm but tinged with irritation. "I've always preferred to support artists quietly, without making it about the money."

Alexi, oblivious to the tension he had caused, raised his glass again, sloshing champagne over the rim. "A true patron of the arts, our Lord Devin!" he declared, still ignorant of the uncomfortable shift in the conversation.

Reese forced a smile, still processing the fact that the man she'd been speaking with all evening was not just an admirer but the one who had significantly influenced her career. "Well, I suppose I should thank you, Devin," she said, her tone thoughtful. "Though I must say, I'm more interested in why you chose my work in the first place."

Devin met her gaze, his expression sincere. "Your work spoke to me, Reese. It had a rawness, a depth . . . something real. The price was irrelevant. It was about supporting an artist I believed in."

Reese nodded, feeling a mix of emotions—gratitude, curiosity, and the lingering impact of Devin's earlier critique. Meanwhile, Alexi, now completely unaware of the gravity of his revelation, was already looking for his next drink.

Although Alexi had divulged a secret, Reese wasn't surprised he had loose lips. She suspected he wouldn't remember telling her who Devin Brooks was. Alexi had also later yapped enough about *Hannah* and its grossly overpriced offer to anyone and everyone he could talk to.

Alexi swayed slightly, a smirk playing on his lips as he

eyed the *Hannah* piece from across the room. "Ah, the *Hannah* piece . . . the one everyone's raving about, right?" He let out a chuckle, clearly amused. He leaned in closer to Reese, lowering his voice as if sharing a juicy secret. "And let's be clear, darling, that outrageous offer? Not from our dear Devin here. Oh, no, someone else decided to play the big spender tonight. A fool with more money than sense, if you ask me." Alexi took a sloppy sip of his champagne, nearly spilling it. "But hey, if they want to waste their fortune on it, who are we to stop them? Just means more spotlight on you, my dear. Though I'd say the real art lies in how you handle this sudden flood of attention." He winked at Reese, clearly enjoying the drama of the evening.

Alexi's words hung in the air, his careless dismissal of *Hannah* stirring something uneasy within Reese. As she listened, her mind began to churn with doubts. Something still wasn't right about that offer, she realized. It nagged at her, the thought that someone, aside from the family would want a portrait of a dead woman.

Sure, the art world had always had its share of morbid fascinations—paintings of old, dead men who had carved their names into history. But those figures had earned their place, whether through power, wisdom, or infamy. Hannah, however, was different. Her rise to this strange form of celebrity had been sudden, born from the grisly circumstances of her death. The public's obsession with her murder was unsettling, and Reese couldn't shake the feeling that this offer was more about capitalizing on that obsession than appreciating the art itself.

As Alexi rambled on, Reese found herself lost in thought, trying to piece together the true motive behind the mysterious bidder's interest.

GOD, OUR WORLD IS FUCKED, REESE REFLECTED AS she gathered herself to open her hotel room door after the long evening. Alexi and Gina were the focus of Reese's thoughts for a while. Gina had gotten sloshed out of her mind, knocked over a table, and damn near got kicked out. Alexi had once again swooped in to save Gina. The actions of Alexi, drunk as all hell, saving an even more faded Gina, echoed in her mind. Gina was always in need of saving. There wasn't a day when she wasn't a damsel in distress. The thought reminded Reese of her first night in Blue Sky.

There had to be a connection; otherwise, Reese couldn't make sense of everything. As she racked her brain, trying to think of people who'd been there that night, she recalled the man sitting in the corner had looked awfully like Devin. But how? How had he gotten to Blue Sky? Wait, the shot of tequila Gina had taken had been sitting on the bar top, waiting for Reese. It was at that moment Reese knew she was a target for more than *Hannah*.

Someone had wanted her to move to Blue Sky, and they wanted to keep her there.

Nineteen

REESE WOKE THE NEXT DAY EAGER TO GO BACK TO
Blue Sky, completely content with running back to her
home, which had seemed like a pipe dream several years
ago. Was she running from her problems? Yes, in a sense.
But she was happy with that.

Reese felt she was living her dream almost every day. She
counted her blessings and even reflected that it was dumb
luck that she was able to follow her passion uninterrupted.
Although her passion might have attracted the wrong eyes
and the wrong attention, Blue Sky was still home.

Before making the trek back up the mountains, Reese
decided to take full advantage of the hotel's amenities,
one of which was a morning pick-me-up: a cup of black
coffee. Reese opened her hotel room door and stepped
forward to leave. Her foot crinkled something, and she
looked down to find a small red envelope. Her heart fell
to the floor.

She couldn't breathe. Reese reached down, hand
trembling. Looking up and down the hallway, she found
nothing and no one. When she opened the envelope, she

was taken aback to see a glossy black-and-white photograph of her and Shance on the couch, their lips almost touching.

Reese's world was once again ripped apart. She recalled the flash that night on the couch, right before Cody had crashed his car into Shance's truck. She remembered Cody screaming about a flash that blinded him. Cody was their only lead! Reese hoped Cody could remember the fine details of that night. She wondered if he even knew he had driven drunk that night. Reese immediately made a call to Shance, who was at her door within fifteen minutes.

She and Shance agreed that getting back to Blue Sky was the best bet to try to talk to Cody before anyone else did—or worse, before the possible stalker and killer got to him first.

Reese had a hard time understanding; she was still unable to grasp what someone wanted with her. Her mind was just as foggy as the morning air. She looked out the window, seeing nothing but a heavy fog that clung to it, causing bits of dew to speckle the glass.

Reese was becoming more and more uneasy as she looked out at the foggy city. Someone was watching her. Looking at the picture of her and Shance, Reese remembered that night, and her insides burned for him.

Reese had to shake herself away from the thought of Shance. She was getting distracted by him. Was he blinding her from the obvious signs? Someone was obsessing over her life. Part of Reese felt hopeless, trapped, waiting to see what was going to happen next. And now the picture had put the final nail in the coffin for her. She didn't feel safe anywhere or with anyone, including Shance, who was now quietly talking on the phone with his head in his hand on the hotel bed.

Reese became more uneasy thinking about going back to Blue Sky. Blue Sky was small, and the chances of catching someone there were greater, at least in Shance's eyes. She started to feel nauseous to the core thinking about the "catching someone" part. Reese wanted to know Shance's plan, if he had one. Part of her hoped there was a chance Blue Sky would erupt with townies flooding the streets with pitchforks to back Shance up.

Reese had spoken to Gina and Alexi yesterday about the plan to get all her art back to Blue Sky. Gina was to have Alexi and the gallery workers load everything into the SUV the following day. Alexi and Gina had made it very clear that they didn't need Reese's help getting everything loaded. Reese doubted that Alexi and Gina were even going to be able to function today, let alone use their bodies to load the art themselves. Reese was tempted to stop by the Sanctuary and see if they were even making an effort to get her art back to its rightful home.

Reese shook off the inclination; she had more important things to worry about, like her life and safety. Why would someone want to harass her in a way that made her fearful for her life and the lives of those around her? Reese now felt Shance was becoming a target just for being around her. Clearly, the second picture showed she and Shance were enraptured with each other's touch. She praised Shance in more ways than she could count. He was a real trouper if he could stick by her through this drama-filled bullshit.

They'd decided that Shance was going to follow Reese back to Blue Sky in his truck. He would head straight to the sheriff's office to get the photo processed. Even now, Reese had a hard time understanding Shance's logic to bring the photo to Blue Sky to get it processed by one of the deputies rather than having it processed in Denver. But Shance knew best, and she was beginning to trust the sheriff—not only with her life, but with her heart.

Before Reese knew it, she was already in her car and ready to make the trek up the gradual mountain passes and sharp turns. Shance pulled in behind her, his dark truck making her Barracuda look like one of the many bugs smashed against his grille.

The damp wintery-fall air surrounded her and Shance as they made their way back to Blue Sky. They finally made it out of the dense city, but the fog didn't lift. In fact, it seemed to grow darker and more ominous as they made their way up one of the many mountain passes they were driving over.

The aspen trees that speckled the mountainsides started changing from a deep green into the fiery yellows and oranges that symbolized the end of the season. The fog seemed to envelop the bright yellow trees, surrounding their pale trunks. The vivid spots of orange, red, and yellow made it look like the fog was attempting to erupt into a flurry of flaming colors.

Reese lost sight of Shance behind her, but that was to be expected, as the fog made visibility harder, and it became near impossible to see. If not for the bright yellow lines on the dark pavement, Reese would question even driving in this dense fog. Something about the fog would make most people feel uneasy, but the dreary dark days made her heart happy. Reese knew most people would pull over and wait out the vapor clouds that seemed to be attached to the mountaintops. There was an echo of danger in her head, but Reese continued on, driving as safely as she could, but also driving anxiously, as she wanted to get back to Blue Sky as soon as possible.

Still, something kept creeping up in her head. She glanced into her rearview mirror, expecting to see Shance's truck, but there was no one on the road besides her. Now that she thought about it, she realized she hadn't seen any car or truck for over an hour. She couldn't even remember when she last saw Shance's truck. She tried to comfort herself, knowing he was still back there somewhere.

Panic squeezed her chest. Her heart started to thud, and the utter feeling of being alone in the dense mountain wilderness hit her like a ton of bricks. Maybe she should pull over.

Just as she had that thought, bright lights surfaced under the thick fog behind her. *It must be a trucker*, she thought. The heavy light bar and ditch lights pierced through the white wall of fog.

Wait.

A wave of fear crashed over her, choking her and tying her stomach in nauseating knots. Those were the same bright lights that had blinded her in the parking lot.

Reese's eyes widened.

This couldn't be happening.

Twenty

AN ALL-OUT FRENZY OF FEAR HIT REESE HARD, AND she felt her life drain from her face. Yes, it was the same truck from the parking lot; there was no mistaking those bright lights and the diesel roaring behind her.

Her foot fell to the floor. The growl of her Barracuda shook her hollow chest. She was going to get out of there one way or another. There was the real possibility that she wasn't going to survive this drive in one piece, but the thought barely brushed past her mind as she hammered harder on the accelerator.

The Barracuda purring up to speed sent Reese deeper into the driver's seat. The feeling of her body being suctioned to the seat, the air nearly being pulled from her chest, was what had made her fall in love with this car from the beginning.

Her fear faded into pure adrenaline.

Reese remembered eyes peering at her and her dad in the passenger's seat, staring at them as they took the first test drive in the 'Cuda, their bodies experiencing that same momentum.

That thought raced past her as she downshifted to gain the amount of horsepower needed to get up the steep mountain pass. The 'Cuda roared in protest as she hammered it again, this time smashing her full weight onto the pedal. Reese's eyes shifted to the rearview mirror, where the truck was fading into the fog. She knew she could outrun the truck—the 'Cuda was *fast*—but at what point would she endanger her life and possibly the lives of others if they were on the same road? Guilt and fear gnawed at her, a mixture only the wicked knew.

The auburn leaves of the aspens whipped past Reese's car, causing the roadsides to seem like they were part of the smoky wildfires that often plagued the mountains. A bright yellow sign also whirled past Reese as she continued to smash the gas pedal. The sign, a familiar one, let Reese know there were sharp turns ahead. She shifted in her seat, gripping the wheel. Knuckles pale as a ghost, Reese shifted again, a decision only she could make. She was going to get away from her aggressor.

Just as Reese reached the corner, the steep drop with metal guardrails alarmed her. She shifted down one, two, three times, making the 'Cuda scream in defiance. The speed of the car physically peeled her out of the driver's seat. Reese moved one hand to the brake deep on the floorboard to the right. Reese pulled it up as she hit the apex of the cliffside. She cranked the wheel with her left hand and turned her head to where she saw her exit.

"*Yes,*" she said as she drifted around the sharp turn like she had practiced so many times with her dad. The fleeting thought of him being proud of her hit her mind for one millisecond before she shifted the 'Cuda again.

Reese released the brake and straightened her wheel. Hopefully that maneuver had bought her some time. Reese eagerly peered into the rearview, where she saw nothing but fog behind her. No headlights pierced through the dense gray day. There was no black truck lurking ominously behind her, ready to wrap her in its web. A wave of joy washed over her as she celebrated the quick-thinking maneuver that had gotten her out of its sight.

As Reese turned to look through the windshield, she screamed. Her eyes went wide, and her hands were unable to take action against the steep turn that was now before her. Reese tried to grip the wheel and gain control before her front end hit the guardrail. Her hands were ripped from the erratic spinning wheel, pain piercing through the adrenaline like a sting from a bee.

The guardrail crumpled in a shrouded metal mass, sending it deep into the 'Cuda's heart. Reese had no time to react, her hands now waving above her head as the vehicle began to roll and flip down the steep hill.

The 'Cuda came to rest at the bottom of the ravine, where a trickling creek made its determined journey through the wreckage.

Time seemed to stand still for Reese before her vision darkened.

Twenty-One

Reese's eyes burned. She blinked, trying to get a clear sight of her surroundings through the blurry fog of her vision. Her ears were ringing, and nothing made sense. Her head was strangely pressurized as she blinked again. This time her vision slowly became clearer. But still, something wasn't right—the sights, the smells, the pressure on her head, and now the stabbing pain in her wrist and stomach.

Reese breathed one shallow breath, then coughed from the gasoline fumes burning her throat.

Gasoline. The familiar smell of a carburetor.

Things started rolling into her consciousness. As they did, the world being upside down and the stabbing pain in her gut made sense. Reese was hanging from her seat belt. The blood rushed to her head, making a heavy pounding pulsate her in her skull. Her car was mangled, the windshield shattered. The crumpled roof reached up, nearly clawing her, letting the stream of water run through the wreckage.

Her arms started to tingle, and she became acutely aware that she had no feeling in her legs. The prickly sensation drove Reese into a frenzy. She grasped at her seat belt, pushing and prodding at the release button.

A familiar noise hit Reese's ears: the sharp crunching of pebbles under someone's feet. Footsteps, and they were coming closer.

Her heart thudded, pulsing in her head. She finally jammed her fingers into the release button hard enough. She splintered her nail apart, causing a sharp pain to wash straight up her right arm into the underside of her shoulder. Her seat belt released. Reese slammed down onto her neck, and the cold stream rushed past her face. The wave of cold brought Reese even more clarity.

She rolled onto her side and pulled her legs from the wheel well. That very action sent prickles down to her toes. She could feel her legs, just barely, but thank god. She knew she wasn't paralyzed from the crash, so the burning pins and needles were a welcome sign. Reese, becoming aware of every sensation—from the cold air hitting her lungs to the pain that seemed to wash over her—was thankful she was alive at all.

She pulled herself toward the shattered window of her car, the glass digging into her elbows and forearms. The movement of getting out of the car wasn't fluid or graceful. She moaned deep in her throat as the splintered glass dug into her skin. Reese pulled herself out of the car, her legs still getting the strange electrical sensation of blood flowing back into them.

Reese managed to get herself out of the car, then fell onto her back, looking at the darkening sky. She wasn't sure where she'd run off the road. She had to be maybe an hour from Blue Sky; that was an hour in a car, of course. If she had to walk, it would be well into the night, maybe even the morning, before she made it back into the sleepy mining town.

Reese became aware of the footsteps coming toward her, the sound of the water sloshing under the heavy steps. She could almost imagine the deep sandy mud squishing out from under the boots that were stalking closer to her.

Reese had to move. She was hoping the person coming toward her was a Good Samaritan who'd witnessed her careen off the cliff. She rolled her head on the damp ground, feeling each and every pebble dig into her scalp. The rich earthy smell hit her nose, making her shiver. She looked to the sound of the person walking toward her, and as her eyes tried to focus on the noise and the figure looming overhead, the sky became dark, the trees seemed to move into the foggy dense hillside, and the cold stream started to become mute.

The night took her.

Twenty-Two

DRIP. DRIP.

DRIPPING FLOODED REESE'S ATTENTION. HER EYE-lids were sticky and rough as she tried to blink away the darkness, but to no avail. Something was putting pressure on her eyes—something smooth, almost silky.

Reese's body came awake as she tried to figure out what the hell had just happened. Pain started flooding through her. Her wrist must have snapped when the wheel was yanked away from her. She thought of the car, the crash. Dread filled her heart.

Why can't I see? Reese pulled her hand toward her face, and the sensation sent shock through her other wrist. They were tied together.

The gravity of the situation changed immediately for Reese as her mind became more and more clear. She couldn't see, and her hands were tied together. She was blindfolded; that was what the silky sensation over her eyes was.

"*Fuck*." She couldn't keep her thoughts straight; all she knew was that she was nearing death by the second. She tried again, clawing at her face. She grasped the blindfold that covered her eyes, then blinked as light blinded her. As her vision settled from the drastic change in light, she looked at anything and everything around her.

The dripping was coming from the corner of the roof. It was raining outside. The damp smell of the forest crept in on her, surrounding her. She was in a dimly lit cabin. The floor was dirt. She gathered every single detail of this place. The walls were old. It looked like a mining cabin that had been left in ruins ages ago.

As Reese moved to sit up, pain in her forearms reminded her that she'd just been in a car accident. The glass was probably still lodged inside her. She wanted to wince in pain, but even moving around caught the attention of a figure, who stalked toward her. Through the shadows, she noticed how heavy and clumsy their feet were. She looked in horror toward the person coming toward her.

"Gina," Reese rasped in shock as she realized that her friend of so many years was the one tormenting her, following her, obsessing over her.

"It's going to be okay," Gina stated as she came closer to Reese.

Reese instinctively moved away from Gina.

"Don't be afraid; you know me. I would never hurt you."

Reese didn't say anything to her; her mind was still trying to understand.

"I saw your car run off the cliff, and I came to save you." Gina's words were quiet, almost out of character from her normal conversations with Reese. She looked at Reese, who sat bloody and in shambles. "Shance called me when you found the photo. I knew I had to come help."

Reese sat in silence, trying to understand what had just happened.

"Look, Reese, I've loved you since I met you, when you first came into the soda shop. I knew at that moment I would do anything for you." She reached out to touch Reese's face.

Reese, like a doe caught in the headlights, didn't move and didn't say anything. She started reflecting on why she'd been brought to Blue Sky: Gina. Gina caressed her face, brushing the slight dew from Reese's sweat to the side.

Reese felt a wave of nausea as the realization hit her, the pieces falling into place with sickening clarity. Gina, the one she thought was her friend, had been manipulating her all along. The constant presence, the subtle touches, the unwavering support—it all took on a darker meaning now. She needed answers.

Reese found Gina touching her as if nothing had happened. Her heart pounded in her chest as she tried to keep her voice steady. "Gina," Reese started, her tone betraying the calm she was struggling to maintain, "we need to talk."

Gina looked up, her face an unreadable mask. "What's up, babe?" she asked, as if this were just another casual conversation.

Reese clenched her fists, feeling the silky ties tighten on her wrists, trying to keep her anger in check. "How long,

Gina? How long have you been lying to me? And stealing from me?"

Gina's eyes widened slightly, but she didn't deny it. Instead, she sighed, as if she had been expecting this moment. "Reese, I was only trying to protect you," she said softly, reaching out to touch Reese's arm. "You were so stressed, so overwhelmed. I just wanted to help . . . to be there for you."

Reese recoiled from her touch, disgusted. "Protect me? By stealing my work and messing with my mind? How is that helping, Gina?"

Gina's expression hardened, a flicker of something darker crossing her face. "I never stole from you." Anger rushed through her words. She continued, collecting herself, "You needed someone, Reese. Someone who understood you, who could see what you really needed. I've always been there for you, and you didn't even notice. You were too busy with your art, your success, to see what was right in front of you."

Reese shook her head, tears of anger and betrayal welling up in her eyes. "I trusted you, Gina. You were supposed to be my friend, not . . . not this."

Gina moved closer, her voice dropping to a whisper. "I am your friend, Reese. I've always been your friend. But sometimes, friends have to do things that others can't understand. I did what I had to do, for both of us."

Reese's stomach turned, the realization that she had been so blind hitting her with full force. "No, Gina. Friends don't do this. Whatever you thought you were doing, it wasn't for me. It was for you."

Gina's face twisted into a bitter smile. "Maybe so. But deep down, you know you needed me. You still do."

Reese moved from Gina's touch, her decision clear in her mind. "Not anymore, Gina. Not like this." What was she going to do? Her hands were tied with a red ribbon, just like her painting. Reese's world shattered as she reflected on her and Gina's friendship.

"Reese—" Gina's voice broke. "Look, I know it doesn't make sense. I wanted to see if you felt anything for me. You saved me at the bar, and I knew then that you loved me. I was so lost before, and you saved me." Gina's delusions began to unravel before Reese. "I wasn't ready to show you how much I love you until now." Gina once again touched Reese's freckled face, tucking her hair behind her ear. That touch, which was once so welcomed in a warm light, had now become the touch that made Reese quiver in fear. "When I drank that shot, I knew I would be in trouble. But you saved me!" Her words were becoming more disillusioned.

For several moments, Gina just stared into Reese's eyes, the look on her face, the person in front of Reese was no longer recognizable. Reese stared in silence, her mind frozen.

Gina stood without warning and stalked in and out of the darkness. When she returned, she was holding a framed picture. Gina turned the picture toward Reese; it was a picture of them when they were kids, sitting outside the Soda Fountain, smiling. "You've been the focus of my entire life, Reese, and I can't wait to see our future together." The words hung heavy in the air.

Still baffled and questioning reality, Reese blinked. She had to get out of there. "Can I see it?" she said, motioning to the picture with her eyes. Gina handed her the photo; it was black-and-white, like the rest.

Reese gripped the photo tightly, pain running up her arm to her shoulder. She pushed the pain down, staring at the photo. Reese swallowed, feeling emotionless about her lifelong friend, who had presumptively killed for her. Reese noted the metal picture frame had ornate edges that jutted out from the corners. A thought whisked by Reese.

Gina moved to sit next to Reese, once again pushing strands of hair away, this time from her neck.

This was her moment. Without blinking, Reese spun toward Gina, raised the picture frame above her head, and drove the corner of the picture into her forehead.

Gina fell backward, screaming in pain.

Reese jumped from the floor and sprinted toward the door. Before she could reach the door, Gina's hand swallowed Reese's ankle, sending her flat to the ground. Reese landed with a thud, the air escaping her chest. She coughed as she began clawing at anything she could reach, once again intently trying to hit Gina, disabling her. Reese fumbled, her hands still tied. Her fingers reached a chimney poker. Perfect. Reese grasped the fire poker and pulled herself upward. With one swing, she smashed it into the side of Gina's head. Gina started wailing in pain and anger. Reese dropped the poker, pulled herself to her knees, and darted to the door, this time swinging the old wooden door nearly off its hinges.

Reese took off into the night, the pattering rain stinging her face. The dark trees seemed to grow larger as she ran through the soggy forest. Each step sent her feet into the muddy forest floor. Reese didn't look back. She didn't know if Gina was coming after her; all she could do was run.

Run faster, she thought. A tree branch whipped past her, clawing at her. She didn't know if she was going in the right direction or if there was even a right direction to go. But still, she ran.

Soon, Reese looked up a small hill, seeing a flat clearing.

It must be a road. Her determination grew exponentially. She ran up the hill, her lungs burning. The wet ground caved under her; one wrong step and she would be sent tumbling back down the hill.

Still, she surged on. As Reese made it to the near top, her ears caught something behind her.

Gina.

Fear welled up inside her. Reese stumbled to find her footing. Gina was gaining on her.

Reese pulled herself up the hill, damn near rolling onto the road. A moment later, Gina pulled herself up onto the road also. Panting in exhaustion, Reese rolled onto her knees. This was it: kill or be killed.

Reese knelt to grip a stone in her still-bound hands, the cold rock weighing her down. She turned in Gina's direction.

Gina was right in front of her. Gina's hand flew right past Reese, grabbing a handful of Reese's soaked hair, making her drop the rock. With the other hand, Gina pulled her arm back and swung her fist against Reese's cheek.

Reese stumbled backward, the pain swelling her face instantly. Her head got light when another blow from Gina's powerful punch rattled her brain. Reese fell to the ground, her eyes swelling shut. Gina's grip ripped through her scalp, peeling her from the ground. Reese screamed out in pain, as she knew this was it.

But before Gina could send her six feet under, a piercing noise broke her screams.

Gina's grip instantly released, and Gina fell to the ground.

Reese pushed away from her, looking to see where the noise had come from. Headlights lit a dark figure, whose hands were steadily holding a pistol. The pistol was still smoking from the shot. Reese crawled toward the figure, still with bound hands, panting in fear.

The steps met her halfway, and the person pulled Reese to her feet, still holding a steady aim toward Gina, who was now gargling strange words at them. It wasn't until she was pushed behind the person that she realized it was Shance. His demeanor said everything she needed to know: stay behind him.

Twenty-Three

THE NIGHT HAD PASSED IN A FLASH, ESPECIALLY considering Reese was in severe physical pain. She was sitting in a hospital bed, groggy from whatever the nurses and doctors had given her. Her wrist was now wrapped in a thick cast. Reese had never broken a bone, so this feeling of her arm being suffocated was new.

A constant concert of beeping came from the machines behind her head, and Reese wondered if everything should be beeping so loud. As her gaze fell on the glass window and hallway outside her pale cream hospital room, a familiar face appeared.

Shance. He was keeping a watchful eye on Reese while talking with uniformed sheriff's deputies. It gave her a sense of peace knowing she was at least near Shance and that he had defended her from her psychotic friend.

Still, the fact that Gina had flown under the radar for so long and not raised any red flags was mind-boggling. Reese was still trying to account for the strange things that had happened, but she couldn't make the connection to Gina. It was at that moment that Reese told herself it had to be true: Gina had admitted it, right? Something inside Reese told her that even after all this, she couldn't see Gina killing for her.

Just like before, saved by the bell, Shance strode into the room, his eyes heavy with a look Reese had never seen.

"How are you doing?" he asked as he made his way to the side of her hospital bed.

Reese looked up at him. Her eyes, dry and heavy like cotton, flickered with confusion. The weight of her disbelief was clear in the way they struggled to focus, as if they couldn't fully process the betrayal that had unfolded before her.

Despite the anger burning inside her, her eyes remained clouded, reflecting the turmoil and the unanswered questions still churning in her mind. All she could do was push everything down. It was too much for her to handle right now, and she decided when it was time to deal with her emotions, she would, but right now was not the time.

"I'm as good as I can be." Honesty poured from her lips whether she liked it or not. "I really don't want to talk about anything. All I know is that my friend for so many years tried to kill me, so forgive me if I don't want to go into details." Reese stared blankly, assuming he wanted to ask her questions about it.

Shance took her hand. "We don't ever need to talk about it if you don't want to. I'll warn you, though, at some point, you'll have to talk to one of my deputies about it. But there's no rush to do this tonight." His undertone suggested that the shot he took had ended Gina and that there was nothing they could do tonight.

Part of Reese felt shame, thinking about how she had lost her best friend. She was conflicted. She had to keep reminding herself that Gina would have killed her if not for the man in front of her.

Finally, after all this time, everything was falling into place inside her. She now knew she wasn't going to let him go; she was falling in love with the man who'd saved her life. Her feelings tonight were all over the place. She blamed the drugs the nurses had given her. What she really wanted was to forget tonight.

"I really just want to go home," she said, squeezing Shance's hand in hers.

Before long, Shance had convinced the doctors to let him sign her out of the hospital on the condition he watch her for the rest of the night and the next day. No doctor would do this for anyone else, but because Shance had demonstrated that he was the most capable person right now, they allowed Reese to leave the cream-colored walls of the hospital.

Shance wheeled her to his truck and lifted her into the cab. It felt like even before Shance could close the door, Reese was drifting to sleep. All she could remember was the clouds to the east becoming light on the winding drive back. Reese drifted soundly to sleep as Shance weaved his way through the mountain roads, back to Blue Sky.

SHANCE GENTLY COOED TO REESE TO WAKE UP. Reese, still blurry from everything, acknowledged him and promptly let her head drop down again.

"Reese, let's get you inside," he whispered again, starting to unbuckle her.

Reese finally woke. This time she planned on at least getting to the couch and drifting off again. Her body fought every moment. Reese didn't want to fight the pain; she let it take her, as she knew sleep was coming soon enough. With Shance's help, she hobbled to the shop door, where she found it unlocked. Weird. She'd locked the shop door before leaving for Denver.

Reese held on to Shance's thin waist as she stepped inside the darkened shop. She reached for the light switch, using Shance as a crutch of sorts.

The lights flicked on.

A gasp hit the dense morning air. As Shance and Reese stood, no words were spoken. They peered up at the lifeless body hanging from the ceiling.

Cody.

His hands were bound to his chest with a red ribbon. His skin was blue gray, and his hair fell in front of his face. His mouth was open wide as if he could still gasp for air.

A black-and-white photograph was bound to his torso, the red ribbon mingling around it. The photo was of Reese downing the glass of wine at the art show just a day prior.

Below Cody's body was a message written in what Reese assumed was his blood. The crimson words would forever haunt her.

"I am always watching."

Epilogue

YES, I WILL ALWAYS BE WATCHING.

He smirked to himself as he looked toward the shop, leaning against the darkened alleyway. He wanted to see the look on her face when she witnessed what he would do for her. Once more, he could no longer help himself; he had to let her know that she was his and no one else's.

Cody had gotten in his way. Cody had seen him the night he crashed his car. In fact, it was his fault Cody had crashed; the flash had nearly blinded him. Cody had watched him standing in the very spot where he was standing now. When he had seen Cody in town, Cody's eyes told him that he knew. He knew it was him. He had killed Hannah, and he did it for her. All for her.

As the sheriff's truck pulled in, part of him wanted to run out and take the sheriff's life for coming between him and Reese. He would do anything for her.

His mouth quirked as he watched the sheriff and Reese step inside.

Cue the stage lights, he thought.

His work was like a damn production. Cody was still hanging there, the ribbon perfectly intertwined with the photo, leading down his legs. Although he still debated now if he should have left the message. It was too perfect. Because like the note stated, he was always watching.

He had seen Gina attack Reese. He'd watched Reese fight for her life. Despite her delicate outward nature, she'd fought like a feral animal. Something about Reese's head being lifted to face him ignited him. And he'd damn near thought Reese saw him in the trees. Her eyes had been swollen, bloody, looking directly at him. He imagined her screaming for his help, but before he could act, the sheriff's shot rang through Gina and right past him. If the sheriff hadn't killed Gina, he would have.

He'd returned to Blue Sky to wait for Reese, and Cody had stridden by him. Cody's stench had nearly burned his nose.

The smell of booze and sex wafted off his body, his pores leaking the stench of sin. He gritted his teeth. This was his chance.

He stepped behind Cody, who was now pissing on the side of Reese's shop. His anger surfaced even more. Cody stiffened upon seeing him.

"You." He pointed at him. "You made me crash my car." His words were slurred, barely decipherable.

He smirked and stepped toward Cody.

"Hey, man, I don't mean no trouble."

He said nothing to Cody, just inched closer.

"What's your fucking issue, Michael?" Cody started to shout.

That was the moment, the second when he lost it. Cody knew who he was; he knew that Michael had caused him to crash his car, and it wouldn't take long for him to figure out he'd killed Hannah. He knew he had to kill him.

He brought himself back to the present, where he saw Reese bury her face in Shance's torso. That same anger rushed through him. As he looked on, his thoughts became clear.

In the hushed embrace of moonlit realms, I am still, a specter cloaked in shadows, my senses attuned to every whispered breath and fleeting motion before me. From my concealed vantage point, I watch with an insatiable hunger, my eyes piercing the darkness to trace each step, each heartbeat echoing in the stillness. They think they've escaped, but they're wrong. I've memorized every detail, every fear etched in their eyes, every tremor in their voice. The lunar glow bathes me in its silver light, a dark shroud that veils my form as I remain unseen, my presence a silent sentinel in the endless dance of night. My purpose, lustful and immutable, drives me onward, an eternal witness to the unfolding drama I created, bound to this eternal watch, forever observing, forever stalking in the moon's embrace. And as they falter in their false sense of security, I smile, knowing that soon they will understand: no one can evade my gaze. I will always be watching.

The sheriff was next.

C. WEHMHOEFER

was born and raised in Colorado, where she developed a deep appreciation for nature. When she's not camping or exploring the great outdoors, she can often be found immersed in her writing or tending to her vibrant garden. She delves into the world of intense and detailed thrillers, crafting narratives that keep readers on the edge of their seats. Her deep connection with the natural world infuses her work with a unique, atmospheric tension, making her stories as immersive as they are suspenseful. An animal lover at heart, C. Wehmhoefer shares her home with her dogs and three cats. However, her greatest loves revolve around her family and her supportive husband, who hold a special place in her heart.

WWW.CWEHMHOEFER.COM

Instagram: C.Wehmhoefer

Printed in the USA
CPSIA information can be obtained
at www.ICGtesting.com
CBHW022102161124
17547CB00012B/815